Love In the A

(A FF Story)

Nika Michelle

Ruff Endz
Some one to
Love
you

This book is dedicated to #TeamFF. You have all been there since book number one and you're still here. Thank you so much. I am so blessed to have such loyal readers.

Nika Michelle

Author's Note:

This book is a spin off from the Forbidden Fruit Series, which includes Bout that Life: Diablo's Story (A FF Prequel), Forbidden Fruit 1, Forbidden Fruit 2: A New Seed, Forbidden Fruit 3: The Juice, Forbidden Fruit 4: The Last Drop and Forbidden Fruit 5: The Final Taste.

If you haven't read the FF Saga, it's okay. You don't have to read it to follow and understand the story. I have added the last two chapters of Forbidden Fruit 5: The Final Taste to give an idea of how Zyon and Mackie's relationship started. It's also a refresher for those who did read FF 5. Thank you so much for the support. Enjoy the ride...

Excerpt from Forbidden Fruit 5: The Final Taste

Chapter 27

Zyon

I was at Daren and Reco's reception decked out in black True Religions and a black and gray button down to match. My feet were adorned in fresh black and gray J's. The platinum Cuban link necklace around my neck stopped right between my pecs. Those long ass chains were out.

My eyes were glued to Mackie's fine ass. That chick wasn't even trying to see me. She gave me the cold shoulder and I wasn't used to that shit. I was used to females trampling over their home girls to get to me. The challenge was what intrigued me, but something told me that I'd still be interested in her if she gave in.

The last time I tried to talk to her she chomped me down. She was fiery and that shit was sexy. It meant that she didn't easily fall for what niggas be spitting. She was strong and that was definitely a turn on. I walked up behind her and whispered in her ear.

"You're still in the A huh? So, it's harder to leave me than you thought."

She turned around to face me with a slick smile. "Are you really still trying?" When she rolled her eyes, I wasn't convinced that she was really annoyed with me.

"I'm gonna keep tryin' until you're mine."

She shook her head. "I already told you that I'm not interested in guys like you. You probably got naked pictures of bitches all in your phone. You flaunt your money and shit and they come running. I'm way out of your league and I'm not impressed by your flossin'. As a matter of fact, you couldn't handle a woman like me. You like weak, needy bitches, so save yourself the time and effort." She turned her back on me and left me to simmer on that.

"Hmm. I think you're worth the time and effort. I don't really like weak, needy bitches. As a matter of fact I'd like to get to know a strong woman who doesn't need me, but you won't let me. If weak, needy bitches are the only ones who give me the time of day, how would I know anything different? What about you take the time and effort to show me the difference? I think it would be worth it," I said not letting her intimidate me with that stand offish shit.

"Wow. Are you so damn sure of yourself that you don't get it? I don't want to…"

I leaned over and kissed her. She smacked the shit out of me. "Why did you do that?"

She was pissed, but I could tell that she liked how forward I was. That shit was a turn on, but she pretended to be offended.

"Because I wanted to. See, as you get to know me more you'll see that I do what I want to do. I don't care how much a person tries to make me change my mind. When I have my mind set on something, I do what I have to do to get it. So, it's not my fault if you tell most niggas no and they give up. They ain't like me. I'm sorry. As a matter of fact, they don't compare to me, but you'll find that out in due time." I looked down at her with so much longing in my eyes.

She just didn't know how much I wanted her and she smelled so damn good. I took in all of her beauty in a short, baby blue dress that hugged all of her curves. It was low cut, so her cleavage literally spilled out. Her round ass was standing at attention and I was staring at it...hard. Damn. Baby was bad. I had to have her and there was no way that I was going to let her keep dissing me. Shit, she just didn't know what she was missing.

She turned around to face me again. Her smoldering eyes had me mesmerized. Damn, she could get anything she wanted from me. All she had to do was look at me like that. I liked the fact that she was so naturally pretty. She didn't need make up. Anything like that was an enhancement. All she had on was some clear lip gloss and a hint of light blue eye shadow.

She licked her lips and I just stared at them as she spoke. "You know what? I'll give you my phone number under one condition?"

"What's that?"

"If you can convince my cousin Tre that you're worthy, I'll give it to you."

I glanced over at Tre. He was sitting down at a table with a cane leaning against it. If I was going by the street code I'd be sizing him up for the fight, but I had mad respect for my nigga Tre. He was my pop's boy, so that made him alright with me. I was sure that I could convince him that I was more than worthy of his cousin.

"After that, if you prove yourself, you'll have to meet my mom. She's even worse than Tre. Don't worry. She's not here. She had to handle some business in VA, but she'll be back."

"So, you're from VA?"

She nodded. "You don't get to find out anything else about me until you talk to Tre."

Her back was turned to me again and I admired her perfect ass as I walked off. Shit, I almost bumped into somebody I was looking at it so hard. Mmm. The things I'd do to her. She just didn't know.

Tre looked up as I sat down beside him. My pops, Deniro, Mel and Ju were sitting with him. Yanna was sitting at another table with Princess, Yanna, Maya and Teji. Reco was sitting at the main table with his bride and the place was filled with Cues, their women and their side bitches. I just knew that if I could pull Mackie she wouldn't have to worry about a side bitch. It would be all about her. I didn't heed my pop's warning. I wanted her and I didn't give a fuck how he or anybody else felt about it.

"Can I talk to you Tre? Alone…"

"Yeah, what's up?" He asked looking like he was surprised at my request.

I looked around the table. My pops, Deniro and Mel got the point and got up.

Once the ears were gone, I got straight to the point. "I'm gonna be straight up wit' you man. I'm really feeling Mackie. She won't give me the time of day unless you approve. I'm not gonna make a plea to you, because I only need to prove myself to her. I can't use my pops as a reference since we just gettin' to know each other. All I can say is I wanna get to know her. If she's the woman I think she is, I'll treat her like a Queen. If not, well, I'll be real wit' her and I'll walk away without breakin' her heart. She's different and that's exactly what I need right now."

Tre shook his head with a grunt. "But are you different? I ain't a perfect man and I don't expect for you to be either. I know that you ain't askin' me for her hand in marriage, but my opinion matters to her. If it didn't she wouldn't have asked you to do this." His eyes traveled over to her and he smiled. "Mackie is special. In a world full of wicked shit, she manages to stay good. She don't need you to corrupt her. I know that you're Blo's son. I respect that. I can tell that you're a real nigga, but I don't really know how you move. Mackie's not a kid anymore though, so since you came over to do what she asked, I approve. Just know that if you hurt her, I don't give a fuck who your pops is."

I had to respect that because it was real nigga shit, so I shook his hand. "I ain't got no reason to hurt her man and I respect where you comin' from. Real nigga shit."

"A'ight young blood.'"

I got up and walked over to Mackie. As I did I looked around at all of the couples in the banquet room. Although I was young, I longed for that. I had never been lucky enough to have a real family. My dad wasn't around and my mom died when I was young. The Cues were the closest thing I had to siblings, so I was searching for something. When I looked at Mackie I felt like I'd found it. The player was in me, but I wanted to change. I wanted something stable with no games.

"Gimme your number," I said aggressively when I was behind her again.

Mackie turned around with a surprised look on her face. She glanced over at Tre and he gave her the thumbs up.

"Don't look so shocked." I laughed as I pulled my cell from my pocket.

She shook her head. "You must've been mighty convincing."

"Your number please. I fulfilled my part of the bargain. Now it's your turn."

She recited her number and I saved it under "Baby."

"A'ight. I'll call you tomorrow. I'm 'bout to get up outta here though."

"Okay." She seemed to be at a loss for words.

I turned to leave and smiled knowing that her number was locked in my phone. Now it was just a matter of time before I finally had the woman of my dreams. My reign over the streets had just begun as the leader of the Cues and it was only right that I had a Queen by my side.

*   *   *

After a week or so of talking on the phone, Mackie finally decided to let me take her out. We were three dates in and I knew that it was time for us to consummate the relationship. I didn't want to rush her, but damn, I wanted Baby bad as hell and she knew that shit.

From our conversations I knew that she wasn't a virgin. She'd had sex before, but she had revealed that she'd never had an orgasm.

"I was with one dude. We were together for three years. We broke up after my freshman year in college because he was so insecure. I guess that was because he never made me cum," she'd said.

I was ready to show her ass exactly what it felt like. "I got that ma. I'll make you cum over and over again. When we make love it's gonna be all about you. Just know that."

"So you're not what they call a selfish lover?" I could hear the smile in her voice.

"Not at all Baby."

I was on my way to drop her off after eating dinner at Chops and grinding at a reggae club downtown. A nigga just knew that he was about to get some of that good shit. Not that it wasn't worth waiting for, I was sure of that. I just felt like I was going to explode already. Looking at her fine ass and hearing her voice was doing something to me.

She held my hand as I drove and I could feel the passion brewing between us. "I underestimated you Zy," she said breaking the silence.

"Oh really?'

"Yeah. I thought that after a few phone calls I'd lose interest, but it's just something about you that keeps me wanting more."

"Hmm. That's what up. You finally opened your eyes to me huh?"

She laughed and then leaned over to kiss my cheek. "Yeah and I'm so glad I did."

"Me too," I agreed.

Just when I was about to turn off on her exit she stopped me.

"You know what? I'm not really trying to go home right now."

A sly smile spread across my face. "Where you tryin' to go?"

"Wherever you're going," she stated bluntly.

Chapter 28

Mackie

As I laid there and basked in the aftermath of the orgasm that he'd promised me, I thought about the fact that it was more like four. He had done things to my body that I didn't know were possible. His tongue was crucial and not only did he make me cum from oral sex, but he'd actually been able to find my G spot in no time. I thought that G spot crap was some bullshit.

I wasn't the type of woman to fall in love quickly, but I was in love with Zy. He was everything that I didn't think he was. The fact that he was so affectionate surprised the hell out of me. His attentiveness to me and how I was feeling was really appreciated. He'd even confessed that he loved me, but I had yet to say it back.

My lack of a father figure had done the opposite of what it did for most girls. I defied the need to fill that void. My mother had taught me that it was more important to focus on myself and my future. I knew that she wouldn't want me with Zy, but I loved him. I was sure of that.

My cell phone rang as I stared at the envelope from Spellman. It was the moment when I'd find out if I had been accepted or not. When I looked at the screen, Zy's number popped up.

"Hey," I said feeling nervous as hell.

"What's up Baby?" He asked. "You okay?"

"Not really. I got the letter from Spellman and I don't wanna open it yet. I'm scared."

"Why the hell would you be scared? You know you got in."

"I damn sure hope so."

"Why don't you wait to open it when we're together? I need you to go with me somewhere anyway."

"Okay," I agreed and my heart leaped in anticipation.

Zy had bought so much excitement to my life and everyday with him was a pleasant surprise. Most of the time it was an adventure.

*   *   *

Zy picked me up and we eventually pulled up to a nice ass high rise in Atlantic Station. I may not have been from Atlanta, but I knew about The Twelve. The exclusive hotel was also where affluent people could rent or buy condos.

I also knew that Atlantic Station was the spot. It was the place where those with money lived, shopped and were entertained. That was the life that I wanted. My question was why were we there?

"What's going on?" I asked as we went inside and rode the elevator to the the 24th floor.

There were twenty six floors in The Twelve and I knew that the penthouses were at the top. Wow. Who did he know with a damn penthouse?

When we got off the elevator I followed him to apartment 2112. I was shocked when he produced a key instead of ringing the bell.

We walked inside and I was immediately mesmerized by how huge the space was. With bright white walls, it was airy, and the huge floor to ceiling windows were the shit. The view was absolutely amazing and I lost myself as I stood there and took in the picturesque scene.

"How do you like this place?" Zy asked as he came up behind me.

He wrapped his arms around my waist and the scent of his Gucci cologne made me feel dizzy. I felt like I was going to pass out when he kissed my neck.

"It's incredible. Whose place is it?"

"Ours…well, if you like it that is."

I turned around to face him and he kissed the palm of my hand. "What…a penthouse? I'm not ready for that Zy…we just…"

He kissed my words away. "You'll be here most of the time, so it's ours. I can't get a spot that you don't like. I mean, you are the woman in my life right?"

"I…I guess." We hadn't actually had the commitment talk yet.

"Okay then. It's official ma. It's you and me, so after I sign the papers you'll get your key. No other woman has ever had a key to my place, so…you gotta know that I'm really feeling you pretty girl." He stared into my eyes as he kissed my fingertips.

"You must be too good to be true. I'm not that lucky." I allowed him to unbutton my top.

"You're more than lucky ma. You're blessed." His smile seduced me as he caressed my breasts. "Do you wanna make love or open that envelope first?"

His mouth was on my skin in no time and as he sucked my nipple, I opted for what he knew that I would.

"Mmm, let's make love first."

*   *   *

Zy kissed my neck right before I got up to get the envelope from my purse.

"Can you open it for me?" I asked as I sat down on the bed. It was crazy that a bed was the only furniture he had in the spot.

He had just bought it and asked me to decorate the place for him. I was excited about that, but it was time to find out my fate.

His soft lips were on my back as I passed the envelope to him.

"Okay," he said and tore it open with no reservations.

I was nervous as hell and I could feel my heart pounding against my rib cage.

He passed the paper to me, but I shook my head. "You read it."

He looked at the paper.

"Mackenzie Braswell, thank you so much for applying to our institution...blah...blah...blah....You have...drum roll please..." he said all dramatically.

I slapped his arm. "Stop. What does it say!"

He smiled. "You...have been accepted to Spellman."

"For real?" I asked with a huge smile on my face. "Are you serious?"

"Dead ass," he said and passed me the letter.

I skimmed over it and jumped up when I saw that he was telling the truth.
        "Yes! Yes! Yes!"

Zy stood up and grabbed me. He spun me around and planted kisses on my lips and then my neck. "Congratulations Baby. I told you that you would get in didn't I?"

        I kissed his neck loving the smell of his intoxicating cologne. "Yes you did."

He pulled away and then stared down at me. "We have to celebrate. I gotta get you something special to commemorate this moment. What is one thing that you really want?"

"Hmm," I thought about it. "You."

He laughed. "Other than me. Something I can buy."

"Oh okay. I want a Michael Kors bag."

He gave me a funny look. "That's it? Damn, you're so different. Most chicks would've had a long list."

"Well, I don't want for much and I'm not like most chicks."

"You're right about that." He stared at me and shook his head. "C'mon. Let's go to Lenox Mall. Your smart ass deserves a shopping spree. Daddy's gonna reward you for making good grades."

There was a huge smile on my face. "I'm not just sayin' this because of the shopping spree, but I love you Zy. As much as I tried not to, I do."

He kissed me tenderly. "And you know that I love you too ma."

*   *   *

After doing some shopping me and Zy stopped at the food court to get some grub. He'd bought me two Michael Kors bags and two wallets to match. One was black and white and one was beige and brown. He also bought me some Dolce and Gabbana Light Blue perfume. Without me even telling him, he picked out my favorite fragrance. He also bought me a few outfits, and some baby blue and white J's so I was smiling from ear to ear. It was obvious that baby blue was my favorite color.

I wanted sushi, but Zy wanted steak, so Prime Steakhouse was the perfect choice. We were sitting there laughing and talking as he strolled through his Instagram page.

"You think you flyy don't you?" I asked as I used my chop sticks to pick up a smoked salmon roll. As I dipped it in teriyaki sauce Zy stared at me.

"What?" I asked feeling myself blush.

"I'm just...I'on know...I'm lovin' this refined shit. I ain't used to it."He kissed my cheek.

"Refined?" I cocked my head to the side. "Okay."

He laughed. "I mean, you know how to use chopsticks. Most chicks I go out wit' don't even know how to use a fork properly."

I couldn't help but laugh too. "Must I keep reminding you that I'm...?"

"Not like most chicks...I know. I can tell." He smiled as he put another piece of steak in his mouth.

"Well, anyway. I don't think I'm flyy. I just got my own swag and shit. You see how fresh I be. Don't front."

"Mmm hmm. I have to go to the little girl's room," I said planting a peck on his lips before I got up.

"You are definitely not a little girl. Now cover up that camel toe. Got me in here ready to hurt somebody and shit. Pull your shit down ma. That thang is too damn fat." He pulled my top down.

I was rocking some stone washed Bermuda shorts with a short sleeved light blue, gray and white plaid shirt tied around my waist. There was a gray sports bra under my white tank top and a pair of white, gray and white J's on my feet. My look was usually casual and comfy, but I knew how to get sexy.

"I'll be back babe," I said with a wink before I sauntered off.

After relieving my bladder, I washed my hands, walked out of the bathroom and headed back to the table. Before I even made it I noticed some chick standing there rolling her neck as she talked to Zy. It was clear that she was mad at him about something. As I got closer I could hear it.

"Oh, so that bitch is your WCW huh? You know damn well I ain't goin' make it that damn easy for you to move on don't you Zy! Do you really think I'm goin' let that little prissy ass, boogie bitch be happy wit' you! If so, you better wake the fuck up nigga!" She had her hands on her hips.

She was about 5'2, thick, with a small waist and big hips. Her skin was the color of milk chocolate and she had hair that fell down to her waist. I could tell that it was real. She was a pretty girl, but I didn't feel intimidated, not one bit.

I made my way to the table and sat down in my seat as if she wasn't even there. When I leaned over and kissed Zy, the bitch just stood there with her mouth wide open.

"For real? You goin' just let this bitch kiss you in front of me? Wow. You're brave just like that bitch." She frowned and tossed her hair over her shoulder.

"Uh, so do you really think I'm gonna keep letting you call me a bitch?" There was a sweet smile drawn on my face. "Don't let the innocent look fool you. I can show your ass a bitch real quick, but this ain't the time nor the place…bitch."

She went off then and her short, dark skinned home girl pulled her back. "Chill the fuck out Kia. You know you goin' get locked up actin' all ghetto up in here."

"Fuck that bitch! Like she better than me or something!"

Zy stood up and got in old girl's face. "Get the fuck up outta here Kia. It's over between us. I broke up wit' you months ago…remember. I ain't goin' sit back and let you disrespect me or my girl. Miss me wit' that stupid ass shit you talkin'. Your girl goin' make a fool out of herself Melanie. You better do somethin' wit' her before I do."

"Fuck that shit! I oughta cut that bitch right the fuck now!" She reached for a steak knife that was on the table, but Zy caught her by the wrist before she could grab it.

"Bye Kia." He picked up the steak knife with his other hand.

"I swear, somebody better come get this bird before I show her ass how real shit can get," I said as if that bitch was not standing right there.

"Chill out ma. I got this," Zy said as he looked over at me. "Melanie, get your girl outta here yo'. For real."

I eyed two men in suits who were making their way over. Kia looked back and saw them and then backed up like she was about to leave.

All I did was keep my arm around Zy possessively. "Be mad bitch. You fucked up and now I got him. Get over it," I taunted her.

"I swear, I'm goin' fuck your ass the fuck up! You better be glad I ain't tryin' to catch a fuckin' case up in this boogie mall bitch! Know that I can still get the dick if I want to. Just know that!"

As they walked out of the restaurant, I simply smirked at her and gave her the finger as I smiled. I didn't give a fuck. Zy was my man and she was done.

"So, that was my ex girlfriend Nakia. She's crazy as you can see. That's why I dumped her fake ass."

When the suits made it over, I knew that it was time to wrap up our dinner.

"Is everything okay?" One of the men asked.

Zy nodded. "Yeah, it's all good. Can we get the check please so we can go?"

He paid for our food and then we headed to the car hand in hand.

"I'm sorry about that shit," he said as he kissed my cheek. "One thing I don't wanna do is bring any drama into your life."

I rubbed his arm. "It's cool babe. If she's acting like that you must be hard to let go of. Too bad that I got you now. Besides, she don't wanna come for me."

"Hmm. I got a feelin' you can hold your own and shit."

"That I can."

"I want you to go to one more place with me. You handle yourself like a real lady and I like that."

He opened my car door after putting our bags in the trunk.

"Where are we goin'?"

"My grandma died a while back and she left me a safe deposit box key. I ain't never had the heart to go see what's in there, but now that I got you in my life, I think I can handle anything. I just want you to be wit' me when I go through it."

"Aww babe…" I gushed. "I feel so special."

"That's the plan ma," he said as he peeled out of the parking lot of the mall.

Epilogue

Zy

"Yanna's pregnant!" My pops yelled over the phone. I had just called him because the shit I had to tell him was really unbelievable.

"That's what's up Pops, for real. I'm happy for you two."

"You don't really sound like it."

I sighed. "I'm sorry. It's just…"

"What is it son?"

I pulled the letter from my pocket that I had found in that safe deposit box. My grandma had left all types of trinkets that my mom wanted me to have. She had been married to this Italian dude named Caruso that I couldn't stand. She had left him when I was nine, but of course he was in and out of her life. He was abusive and at times I felt like he would kill me and her.

I remembered him telling me that he was going to kill me if I kept looking at him like that. It was times when I contemplated how I was going to kill him. My mother sent me to Atlanta to stay with my grandmother soon after. After reading that letter, I knew why. She had tried to save my life, but I had wanted to stay to save hers.

"It's something my grandma left for me. A letter my ma told her to give me when I was old enough. I wanna read it to you," I said trying my best to contain my emotions.

"Okay, but first, I'm glad that you're doing right by Mackie. I told you to stay away, but who am I to step in the way of love right?" He chuckled. "Tre told me that she's happy wit' you. That's all that matters. Take it from me. When you find the right one you know it. Don't fuck it up for that random pussy that ain't worth it. I'm tellin' you from experience," my pops advised.

I took his advice to heart. "No doubt man. So, you know for sure that I'm gonna have a lil' brother or sister?"

"Yeah man. Yanna got sick in France and I took her to the ER. We thought it was food poisoning, but she's pregnant. We had it confirmed," he said sounding all happy. "She's not quite a month yet, but it's real this time."

I smiled. "That's what's up Pops. Tell Peanut I'm gonna come scoop him this weekend and tell Yanna congrats."

"A'ight. Now read the letter man."

"Zy, if you're reading this, I must be gone. I knew that Caruso would do it. He kept threatening to, but I couldn't let him hurt you. I didn't know how to protect you. You were so young and innocent and I didn't want you to keep being exposed to my bullshit. My first mistake was your father, now him. Believe me, you are the only thing in my life that wasn't a mistake. Your grandma is probably so ashamed of me. I sent you away because I had to. I don't know what you remember, but you probably know how violent Caruso was. He's a dangerous man and he's tied to the mafia. I would never want you to go after him, but I am sure that if you're anything like your father you will. I

love you son. Look after your grandma and be good. Know that you were my top priority and I'm sorry for leaving you. Your mom."

There were tears in my eyes as I held on to her wedding ring. "I gotta go to New York and find him. I gotta kill that nigga for killin' my mama. I knew that bullshit fire wasn't an accident."

"Zy, look, I'm sorry that I wasn't there. If I had known about you, I would've held you down and shit. You know that. If you wanna find that mufucka I'm wit' you. Shit, I owe you that much. I know how it feels to lose your mom. If I hadn't been able to kill those niggas that night I would've hunted them down until I did," Diablo said letting me know that he was in my corner one hundred percent.

"Thanks Pops. That's what I was hopin' you would say. It's on then. We 'bout to take a trip to NY."

"That's what it is then. Call me later and let me know what's up."

"A'ight. I gotta get back to Baby anyway," I said and snuggled up next to her.

Damn, a nigga had found love in the A, but I also found out the truth about my moms. Before I could move on with the love of my life, I had to avenge the murder of the first woman that I loved.

Love In The A

Prologue

Yonkers, NY

Summer 2001

Zyon

"You think it's that fuckin' easy to leave me bitch?"
Caruso's loud voice resonated inside of the small
apartment like sub woofers blasting through the hood.
"Like I didn't know that you would bring your ass right
back here!"

The familiar smell of his Cuban cigar permeated the
air around me as I crouched behind the sofa so that he
wouldn't see me. It wasn't because I was afraid of him. I
was used to him hitting me and my mother throughout their
entire five year relationship. They were only married for a
year before she fled back to Yonkers with me in tow. She
was originally from Brooklyn, but had moved to Yonkers
when she was pregnant with me. When she left Caruso she
went right back to the neighborhood she lived in before she
had met him. Of course that was a stupid move. Like he had

said, he knew that she would go there. That was where her sister and best friend lived.

I was in position as I got ready to stick the knife that I was holding in whatever body part I could reach on him. At the age of nine, my mom had tried to protect me from the influence of the violent streets, but she had brought violence into our home. Since the moment that she met Caruso, both of our lives had changed for the worst. I had no clue that he would be the reason that my life changed forever. My naïve mind had convinced me that I'd always have my mother, but I was wrong as hell.

"Get out of here Caruso! I filed for divorce! What is the point of us being married any way! All you do is beat me and make my life a living fucking hell. I won't let you keep doing that shit around my son! If you don't get out, I'm calling the cops!" The cordless phone was in her hand and she was clutching it for dear life.

I didn't know the real reason she never called them. I knew that she was scared, but it wasn't enough to make her call. Maybe it was because she knew the repercussions of calling the cops on a man like Caruso.

"I ain't going no fuckin' where! I told you to send him to live with his grandmother, but you insist on keeping his ass! All he does is eat, sleep and shit!" Caruso yelled with his fingers around her throat.

She fought to loosen his grip from her neck. "He's my son and he's only nine! I'm not sending him away for you! Look at how you treat me! Your family doesn't even know about us. They don't know that I exist because you can't openly be with a black woman. Well, I don't want to be your secret anymore. I'm tired of it! I can't be with you Caruso and I'll never choose you over my son! You can do whatever you want to me, but I won't let you hurt him anymore!" Tears fell from her eyes and I felt my own eyes start to burn.

Her beautiful face was always full of stress, and I hated to see my mom look like that. She was all that I had since I'd never met my father. As I stared up at her tear streaked face my heart swelled with love. All I wanted to do was see her smile again. Caruso never made her smile. All he did was make her cry, so he needed to be eliminated from her life. I wanted to do that for her, but I was too small. Although I had the heart to do it, I couldn't do it with my bare hands. I needed a gun, but how would I get one? My mother didn't have a gun. I knew that Caruso had one. I'd seen him pull out guns plenty of times. A few times he'd pointed them at my mother for disobeying him. That would be followed by threats to kill her and a severe beating that lasted for hours. Sometimes I would get beat too.

I watched as the olive complexioned man with the sleek, dark hair, sinister eyes and tall, slender frame removed the belt from the waist of his black slacks. One thing I did know was that Caruso was a man who was feared in the streets. He was a high ranked member of the Italian mob who ran a drug cartel based in Brooklyn. Most grown men were afraid to stand up to him, but my heart didn't even skip a beat at the thought of stabbing him to death. Maybe I wouldn't be able to kill him, but I had to stop him from beating her.

The first strike of the belt made the buckle hit her in the face and she yelped out in excruciating pain. "Caruso no! Stop! Please! Not in front of my baby!"

She didn't see me, but she knew that I was there somewhere.

"Fuck that little nigger bastard! I'll kick his ass too!" He yelled as he beat her across her body mercilessly

with the thick leather belt. My reaction was to bolt toward Caruso and attempt to stick the knife in his leg with all of my strength. I wasn't as strong as my desire to hurt him though. The knife barely even went through the muscle of his thigh, but I did manage to get him away from my mother. The knife was still partially in his leg when he turned around with wrinkles in his forehead and a mean ass scowl on his face.

"You little black motherfucker!" He growled.

He picked me up by my arms and then tossed me into the mahogany wood coffee table. I felt the side of my face hit it so hard that it knocked me out cold.

*   *   *   **

I came to in the hospital. My mother sat beside my bed and held on to my hand as she cried. There were bruises all over her face from that belt buckle. Although I was young, I wondered what she had told the doctor. Did she finally tell the truth? Was Caruso finally locked up behind bars? I could only wonder how she got away from him to get me there.

"I'm sorry baby," she managed to choke out along with her sobs. "But you can't be trying to protect me. You're not big enough yet."

I only nodded because I couldn't talk. I wanted to tell her that I would always try to protect her. My jaw was wired shut and my face was covered with bandages, so I couldn't say a word. There was no pain at the moment, but that was only physical. The mental pain and anguish of seeing my mother hurt over me along with her other pain was too much. As the tears slid from my eyes, my heart was aching for her. There was no way I could keep letting her live like that, but what could I do? I felt so helpless. My only attempt at saving her life had resulted in me almost losing mine.

I had also suffered from a severe concussion, but none of that had stopped me from wanting to remove that dangerous man from my mother's life. After I recovered she sent me to my grandmother's house in Atlanta while she got herself together. I had overheard my mom tell my Aunt Brittney that Child Protective Services had threatened to remove me from her custody if she didn't. She'd managed to elude Caruso, but nobody knew for how long.

My grandmother stayed up late at night praying out loud in tongues and anointing me with praying oil while I was in Atlanta with her. She wasn't aware of what my mother was really going through, but she could sense that something was wrong. My mom made me promise not to say anything about it to her, so out of loyalty and love for her I didn't. Instead I told my grandmother that I had an accident on my skateboard.

I returned to New York for school and my mother had got an apartment in Brooklyn. She also had a job cleaning up office buildings. Things were peaceful for a little while, but Caruso always found her. Each time the urge to kill him became stronger and stronger. There was never a time that I didn't try to keep him from hurting my mom. She didn't raise me to be in the streets, but they were calling me. Caruso taught me two very important life lessons that I vowed to live by when I was grown up. Number one was to never put my hands on a woman. Number two was to never bow down to any man. I promised myself that once I got some size on me any man who came at me wrong was going to get dealt with permanently.

After almost two straight years of peace, Caruso found my mother again. Of course I was sent to spend the summer with my grandmother soon after. I never saw my mother's face again after that summer. Deep down in my gut I knew that Caruso had killed her, but at the time I had just turned twelve. Everybody kept telling me that her death was an accident. She had supposedly left a pot burning on the stove when she went to sleep. When I thought about the man who I'd witnessed hurt my mom over and over again, I wanted to blow his brains out. I often dreamed about ending his life.

*   *   *

2011

ATL

Now that I was a man, and a powerful one at that, I knew how to fight like a boxer and shoot a gun like a pro. Every time I beat a nigga's ass, or shot a mufucka I saw Caruso's face. A nigga wasn't going to be small and insignificant forever and he should've known that shit. As I held my .44, I stared in the mirror at the faint scar that was left on my cheek to remind me of the man whose life I had marked ten years ago. I was going to kill Caruso before I took my dying breath and that was word on my life, the woman that I loved and my unborn seeds.

Chapter 1

Zyon

"I already told you that you don't have to work Baby. I want you to just concentrate on school. What the hell? You don't trust a nigga. I'm tryna show you how I feel about yo' fine ass," I said as I reached up to place the .44 in the top of the closet.

We were at my new spot at The Twelve, so I liked to keep that street shit away from her. From what I knew her mom and pops were heavy in the streets, so I wanted to show her something different. Her pops had been murdered and her mother had tried to keep her sheltered from what the street life had to offer. Mackie's mother kind of reminded me of my mom, but look at how I had turned out. So far her moms had done a good job though, but Mackie was no fool. She was like a diamond in the rough. Her edges were a little jagged, but she was undeniably beautiful. My girl was a gem and I was going to remind her of her worth every day of her life. That was my word and my word had always been my bond.

"I know what you told me Zy, but I'm used to workin'," she said as she sat down on the bed. "I've already applied for some jobs. I hope I get a call back from

Verizon. They need customer service reps at their call center in Dunwoody."

She was texting somebody on her iPhone and I figured that it was one of her girls back home in Richmond. Well, at least that was what I hoped. We'd only been together for a month, so I didn't know what competition I had out there. All I knew for a fact was that she didn't have any.

"But you don't *have* to work ma. I already told you I got you. What part of that shit don't you understand? You act like I'm talkin' in German or some shit," I said as I closed the closet door and then turned to face her.

I could tell that she wanted to say something, but she didn't. Instead she turned to break her eye contact with me.

"What's wrong?" I asked before sitting down beside her.

When I leaned over to kiss her cheek she moved away.

"My mama warned me about guys like you. The same thing happened with her and my daddy. He told her that she didn't have to work so he could control her. I ain't lettin' no man control me Zy. I love you, but I'm my own woman. I appreciate the things you do for me, but if I rely on you what's gonna happen if your lifestyle takes you away from me? It'll be better for me not to depend on you."

I nodded as I held her hand in mine. "Okay, I understand why you would feel that way, but just know that nothing will take me away from you. If you want to work that's fine. I don't wanna control you. I love that you on your independent shit. I just need you to know that you workin' is a want and not a need."

She nodded, but her look was apprehensive. It was like she was having second thoughts about being with me.

"Okay?"

She looked up at me and said, "Okay."

"You havin' doubts about us?"

"I don't even know what I'm feelin' right now Zy," she said with a sigh. "You haven't even met my mom. Tre may have approved, but I know that she won't. She'll be here next week and my...damn, my nerves are bad. She wants me to meet a doctor or lawyer, get married, move into a gated community and have lots of babies. In other words, she wants my life to be the total opposite of hers. I think being with you will make her look at it like I'm repeatin' her history," she explained still not making eye contact with me. It was like she thought her words were hurting me. They were, but I couldn't help but understand where she was coming from.

"You ain't repeatin' history. You're you and I'm me. We ain't your folks ma, so let that shit go. Besides, you're a grown ass woman and you don't need your mom's approval to be wit' me. If you love me you love me. Nobody or nothing can change that. If she don't like me it's because she ain't give me a chance. Just like you almost did at first and even you admitted that that was a mistake." I couldn't help but kiss her pouted lips.

"You're right." She sighed, but still looked like she was feeling some type of way.

"C'mon Baby. Don't look like that." I moved her chin up so that she was looking at me. "Why you goin' do a nigga like that?"

"What?" She asked like she didn't know what I was talking about.

"You lookin' like bein' my woman is makin' you so damn miserable. It ain't that bad is it?"

She smiled. "It's not bad at all Zy. I'm just…fuck it. It doesn't matter. I love you and you love me. That's all that matters, right?" When she leaned over and kissed me I knew that the conversation ending didn't make the issue done with.

I nodded. "Right, but do you have to convince yourself to be wit' me? What's goin' on in your head Baby? Tell me what's changed 'cause…"

"Nothing's changed Zy." She grabbed my hand and placed it in hers. "I know how I feel, but that doesn't mean that those on the outside looking in will understand it."

"Those on the outside lookin' in need to stay right there on the outside and mind their own fuckin' business." I pointed to me and then her. "This is us. And it ain't shit that'll keep us from bein' together if we don't let it," I protested. "I finally got you and I ain't gonna let you go."

She shook her head. "Zy, it hasn't been that long. You can't possibly feel that way. I mean what if I'm not what, or who you expected me to be? What if…"

"Shhhh, it ain't no what ifs. I know what I want and I know who I want. It's you, so don't start wit' that doubtin' and shit. I don't know who you been listenin' to, or what's been goin' on, but I knew since the moment I laid eyes on you that it was over for a nigga. I can't explain it and I don't need to. Just relax and let shit happen the way it's supposed to. I ain't just sayin' shit to get in your head, or to get some pussy. I don't need to do that ma. I don't play games. I'm a grown man and you ain't no lil' girl. A'ight. Don't try to figure me out. Be patient wit' a nigga ma and everything else will fall right into place. Damn. You act like we got a crystal ball and shit."

"You know that you're very convincing right?" She asked with a satisfied smile on her face. Why did I feel like it was only temporary?

I nodded knowing that I was a manipulative ass nigga. "Hell yeah," I agreed. "Now let's go. My pops invited us to his crib for some grub."

"A'ight," she sighed and got up to follow me.

*   *   *

I had always known who my father was by name but I had just had the chance to meet him recently. His name was Diablo and although he was now in what he called "retirement", he was one of the most ruthless, venomous gangstas the A had ever seen. I'd heard so many stories about him when I first joined the Cues. My pop's father and Uncle started the Cues and the Kings had always been their biggest rival. When I joined the Cues almost four years ago everybody thought my pops was dead, but for seven years he'd been hiding out in Miami to avoid a federal drug indictment. He even took over the drug game there as his alter ego Polo Loco.

The day we officially met there was a shoot out between the Cues and the Kings at his crib. He felt like I had heart because of how I was out there bucking like a G. After that he invited me on a big drug and money heist in Miami. We took over five hundred keys of coke and a hundred million dollars from some Columbians. I'd even threatened to take his life that night, which resulted in him and his wife Ayanna finding out that he was my father.

I wasn't going to kill him, but I was mad that he had never been there for me. I'd snapped, but when Ayanna put a gun to my head for pulling out on her man, that shit gave me a reality check. Since then we'd bonded and found out for a fact that I was his son through a DNA test. Now we could finally make up for lost time.

Pops was frying up some trout and tilapia with hush puppies, coleslaw and homemade French fries. Damn, damn, damn. A nigga was ready to throw down. Two weeks had passed since I'd called him to read my late mother's letter over the phone. Neither of us had brought it up since. I didn't want to keep putting it off, but he didn't want to bring up our impending trip to New York to Yanna and I didn't want to cause any more complications between me and Mackie by leaving. She was already acting like she didn't want to fuck with a nigga like that. Still, the need to kill Caruso was coursing through my veins like no urge I had ever felt before. It was even stronger than my new found love for Mackie.

Yanna, Princess, Daren and Maya were sitting by the pool with their feet in the water when Mackie decided to kick her sandals off and join them. Pops was still cooking and the kids were running around playing in the front yard. Tre, Reco and Ju were sitting in front of the huge 78 inch flat screen in the living room watching an Atlanta Hawks and Miami Heat game. It was approaching time for the play offs so they were hyped up.

"Who's winnin'?" I asked as I made my way over to them.

"The Heat's kickin' ass," Tre said as he pounded me up.

I did the same with Ju and Reco before my attention shifted to Diablo. "Yo Pops, can I holla at you real quick?"

"Yeah, what's up?" He asked as he headed to the kitchen.

I followed and helped him set the food up on the counter. "Man, I'm really feelin' Baby, but it's like she's havin' doubts about a nigga. What do you think I should do to let her know that I'm serious about her? She thinks I don't want her to work to control her, but I just want to take care of her."

He cleared his throat and then went to the fridge to grab a Corona. "You want one?" He asked.

"Yeah," I said and reached over to take the beer bottle that he passed to me. It didn't matter that I was eighteen and would be nineteen in a few months. He already knew that a nigga had been drinking for a while and there was no need to try to change me.

He sat down on a bar stool and I sat beside him.

"If she wants to work that's a good thing. It shows that she's independent and ain't usin' you. Look, you and Mackie are both young as fuck, so it's normal for her to have her doubts about ya'lls relationship. She lost her pops before she even got the chance to know him, so she probably has a hard time trustin' men to be there anyway. You just have to go out of your way to erase her doubts. It's gonna take some time, but if she's worth it you'll do what you gotta do," he said before getting up to look in a drawer for something.

He made his way back over to me and put a key in my hand. "This is the key to my spot on Lake Lanier. As a matter of fact it's yours now. Take your girl there for a romantic weekend. The more you do to prove yourself the more she'll see how serious you are. Then she'll put her trust in you. Eventually she'll relax and let you lead."

"A'ight," I said with a nod as I thought about my woman. She was everything I was looking for and there was no doubt in my mind about that fact. I just had to make it my business to prove it to her.

When I looked up my pops was giving me the side eye.

"What?" I asked wondering why he was looking at me like that.

"You in love young buck?" The expression that he wore was one of pride.

I smiled. "Yeah man."

He chuckled. "Is it mutual?"

I nodded. "She said she loves me."

"Who said it first?"

I grinned.

"What?"

"Yeah man. I had to let her know how I feel."

"Let me find out that you ain't nothin' like your old man. Shit, at your age all I wanted to do was get some pussy. I wasn't thinkin' 'bout no love."

"Hmm, I heard about you," I said with a sly grin on my face. "My mom told me all about how you played her and shit."

"I never played your moms man. That's my word. I told Niley from day one what kinda nigga I was. One thing about me was I ain't never tried to play nobody. I let chicks know up front that I wasn't that dude who was gonna settle down. I tried the relationship thing once after her, but it didn't work out and then I met Yanna. I fell in love wit' the one I was meant to fall in love wit'. Don't get me wrong. I hate how things played out wit' your moms. If it was up to me I would've been in your life and shit. Now I know that it don't matter how old you are, it's just up to the man. When the right one comes along it is what the fuck it is. If you know you love her do right by her. Don't dog her out if you really care about her Zy. I know how it feels to be wrong as hell and to hurt someone who really loves you. It's selfish and it ain't nothin' like feelin' like the woman you love is done wit' your ass. If somewhere down the line you realize that she ain't the one, or you wanna play the field, just be real wit' her man. That's my nigga's fam and shit. I don't wanna have to bust a cap in my nigga 'cause of you. Shit would get real so fuckin' quick."

"I ain't tryin' to do nothin' but love Baby, for real. I got mad respect for her. I'on wanna cause no problems. Thanks Pops." I was grateful as I looked at my father. The man I'd longed for my whole life.

"Anytime son." When he reached over and wrapped his arms around me, I had to contain my tears. There was a real bond between us and it was one of those moments I'd wanted for so long.

*　　　*　　　*

Mackie

"I swear ya'll youngins and ya'll phones," Princess said as she shook her head at me.

I couldn't help but laugh. "Damn you sound old as hell."

She playfully shoved me. "Watch yo' mouth lil' girl."

I pretended to almost drop my phone in the pool. "Ooops! Let me stop before I drop it for real."

"If you drop it in there your lil' boo thang just gon' buy you another one," Daren said with a smile on her face.

"I know right," Maya added. "He ain't gon' let you go without talkin' to him for too long."

"You done snagged Young Blo," Yanna shook her head. "Mmm, good luck with that if he's anything like his father."

Maya, Princess and Daren laughed. I had no clue what kind of man Diablo was. All I knew was that he seemed to treat Yanna like she was a queen, but I had no idea what she had to go through before he got to that point. Princess had often told me about how Tre had been before he was husband material. I didn't know if I had that kind of patience. As much as I loved Zy in such a small amount of time, I would have no problem dropping him if he showed his ass. I didn't have time for that shit. The drama I'd already been through with his ex was enough. I didn't have time for anything else, because I had to stay focused. My education and future were far more important than love.

"What does that mean?" I asked with a confused look on my face.

Yanna shrugged her shoulders. "Nothing hon. It's just that I had to go through a lot before Diablo finally realized what he has. Now, Zy and Blo are two totally different people, but I can tell that Zy is a lot like him in some ways. Just be careful. What comes with men like them can be a bit much for the average chick to handle."

I thought about what she had just said. "I'm far from average," I spoke up confidently.

Yanna nodded in approval. "That's what's up then shawty. You might be able to handle that lil' nigga then."

I was smiling until I came across something on Facebook that altered my mood. The smile on my face disappeared instantaneously.

That bitch Kia had posted pictures of her and Zy on her page and tagged him so I could see them. I took it that he hadn't seen them yet, because she'd just posted the pictures ten minutes before I logged in. What the hell was that bitch's problem? She was trying to piss me off and that shit was working. There were three pictures that I assumed had been taken when they were together. They were kissing in one of the pictures and I was fuming inside.

"That fuckin' bitch!" I yelled and stood up to go inside.

I had to show Zy how out of pocket his ex skank was being. If I knew where to find that bitch I would've gone and punched the shit out of her for disrespecting me. She knew that I would see those pictures. The fact that Zy and I were openly in a relationship didn't stop her from trying to cause some more damn drama. I had a feeling that heifer wasn't going to stop until my fist made contact with her big ass mouth.

"Zy!" I called out after going in the house.

I caught my breath in awe because the place was so beautiful. There was a moment when I almost said wow out loud as I looked up at the winding mahogany stairs.

"What's up Baby?" Zy asked as he came up behind me and wrapped his arms around my waist.

It was like I was stuck in a trance as I stood there in the foyer.

"This house is beautiful," I said breathlessly as I turned to look at him.

He grinned. "I would say thank you, but it ain't mine." Suddenly he had a straight face. "What's wrong?"

I sighed and then showed him what Kia had posted. "You need to control that bitch before I…"

"I'll handle her. There ain't no need for all that. A'ight?" He tried his best to calm me down. "Those are old pictures Baby."

I sighed in frustration. "I don't care Zy! This shit right here is the reason I don't do relationships! I don't have time for the drama that comes with them. There are things I want to do with my life and they don't include throwing it away over some nigga!"

"What?" He looked hurt. "So I'm just some nigga to you?"

As I ran my fingers through my hair I thought about how confused I felt. I hadn't even known Zy that long and I was already head over heels for him. How the hell had that shit happened so fast? One minute I despised him and I was in love with him the next. The thing was I had been feeling him all along, but men like him scared me. I was afraid that his lifestyle would derail everything that I'd worked so hard to accomplish. Why would I digress when my life had been all about progression? I didn't want to disappoint my mother or myself for that matter, but when I was with Zy it felt like he was worth the risk.

"No, you're not just some nigga. I'm sorry for saying that. It's just that…I don't know. I'm so damn confused right now."

"Let's go upstairs and talk and then we'll come back down to get something to eat," he said right before leading the way up the stairs.

I followed him into a bedroom with pale yellow walls and a queen sized bed covered in a white and yellow blanket. It was clearly a guest room, so I felt comfortable sitting on the bed. Zy closed the door and locked it before sitting down beside me. He held my hand in his and stared into my eyes.

"I love you Baby. I have since the first moment I laid eyes on you in that hospital waiting room. It was over between me and Kia way before then. For a little while I thought I cared for her, but I realized that she wasn't the one for me. I wanted more than she could offer. You're different and I know now that shit didn't work out wit' her because she ain't you. I know it. When I look into your eyes I'm convinced that I'm one of the lucky ones who found my soul mate sooner than most. I just need you to be on the same page as me."

When he leaned over to kiss me I couldn't help but let his tongue part my lips. As we kissed his warm, strong hand made its way up to my breast. When he squeezed and then softly twisted my nipple, I was instantly wet. I had to ignore my physical attraction to him and put my foot down despite how hard it was.

"I love you too, but I will not sit back and let some bitch from your past disrespect me. I expect you to let her know, or I will. Handle that bitch Zy. If you don't I'm going to assume that you still give a fuck about her and in that case you can kiss my ass goodbye." I had an attitude, but when I thought about those damn pictures I felt some type of way.

He kissed me again and then softly sucked on my bottom lip before pulling away. "I'm gonna handle her right now Baby."

I sat there and watched as he pulled his phone from the pocket of his jeans. First he removed the tag from the pictures that she had posted, and then made a call. He put the phone on speaker and we both waited as it rang.

"Yeah, now you wanna call a bitch," that hoe answered in an annoying high pitched voice.

I rolled my eyes in annoyance. Damn, I wanted to say something bad as hell, but he told me that he would handle it. As much as I didn't want to, I had to respect that shit. If it wasn't handled after that, I was going to have to do what I had to do.

"What the fuck is your problem yo'?" He asked with a frustrated frown on his face. Damn that shit made his fine ass look even sexier.

"I ain't got no fuckin' problem nigga. You're the one who seems to have a problem rememberin' how good shit was between us. I had to remind your ass."

I shook my head and rolled my eyes again. He could sense my agitation so he put his pointer finger to my lips and mouthed, "Chill ma. I got this."

Instead of cussing that bitch out I nodded and let him handle her ass.

"There ain't no us shorty, for real. I wish you would just accept the fact that whatever the fuck you wanna call what we had is over. I moved on and it would be a good idea if you did the same. I don't need you lurkin' around and pissin' my lady off and shit."

"Wow, that lil' innocent act that bitch is playin' got you wide open and shit." She laughed like she'd said the funniest shit in the world. "I never thought I'd see the day that your so called hard ass would be dumb over some bitch."

I opened my mouth to say something, but Zy shook his head.

It was hard for me to stay quiet, but I did.

"Don't call her a bitch. Like I said ain't shit happenin' between us ma. I'm wit' Baby now and I ain't gon' let you or nobody else disrespect her. I don't need you to post pics on my page to remind me of a gotdamn thing. I remember everything, especially how triflin' your ass is. You fucked my nigga Cam for a Molly right after I hit. You ain't think I knew 'bout that shit huh? I don't wife rachets. I told your hoe ass that, but you ain't listen. You thought your pussy was that good ma?" He laughed. "I got news for you shorty. Pussy ain't enough and it comes easy for a nigga like me. I prefer selective pussy though. You probably don't know what the fuck that is, so let me break it down for you. Selective pussy is that premium pussy that ain't been all ran through and shit. Selective pussy is between the legs of a woman who is picky about who she fuck, but you wouldn't know shit about that. You got that community pussy and I don't want no part of that shit no more. I don't like sharing. I'm a stingy nigga. So, wit' that said, delete my number and act like you ain't never meet me. If you don't…"

"You wit' Baby now?" Kia laughed mockingly. "Nigga bye. I don't give a shit about that bitch! Believe that! I'm gonna fuck wit' that prissy bitch just for the hell of it nigga! I'm gonna make her wish *she'd* never met you! You won't even be worth it once I'm done wit' her ass! Fuck your threats nigga! Shove 'em up that boogie bitch's ass! Like I told you before, I ain't gon' just sit back and let you be happy wit' that bitch! Get used to it!"

She hung up before I could get my two cents in and I was mad as hell.

"Fuck that! I ain' t gon' let that damn bird bitch talk shit about me like that!" I jumped up from the bed. "Take me to whoop that bitch's ass! Fuck talkin' and shit!"

He stood up and pulled me into his arms. "She ain't worth it ma." When he pulled away and stared into my eyes I could feel my anger dissipate. "You're the one that I want. She don't mean shit to me."

"I just can't stand bitches like her. They just don't know when to move on. You told her you don't want her. Damn." She sucked her teeth.

He kissed my forehead. "She'll get over it. Now, let's go get something to eat."

"Okay," I said with a sigh before following him out of the room. I had a feeling that shit with Kia wouldn't be that easy, but I wanted to believe that it would. Maybe by some miracle she would just get over it. How much of her bullshit would I be able to take before I snapped?

I had never been the type to fight over a dude, but I would beat a hoe down for fucking with me. If she knew what was good for her ass she'd leave me alone before I showed her what kind of woman Sylvia Braswell had *really* raised.

Chapter 2

Zyon

Before my weekend with Baby I had to make sure that shit was straight on the streets. I was a money making nigga first and foremost. The Kings were no longer a threat to our operation, but that didn't mean that there weren't other crews out there ready to take their place on our shit list. The Cues were dominating the drug game and everything appeared to be as it was supposed to be in the hood. If somebody wanted to gun for our position they could bring it, but their chances of winning the top spot were slim to none. There was no way in hell I was going to let go of my reign over Atlanta. As far as I was concerned a nigga like me needed more territory. I wasn't just satisfied with running the A. I wanted to run Georgia. Fuck that I wanted to flood the whole East Coast. Shit, the Cues had enough money and product to do it.

I met with Deniro, Mel and and my nigga Cane at the "boardroom". That was our headquaters on Candler Rd. Cane was my right hand man because he was close to my age and the first nigga I'd met before joining the Cues. He was like a recruiter in my hood and his references to my pops let me know that running the Cues was my calling. When I heard the name Diablo, I already knew what that shit meant. Although I knew that he was my pops, I had kept that shit to myself. Shit, I knew those niggas wouldn't believe me and at that time we thought he was dead. I worked my way up the ranks and just like I thought, all things happened in due time. Now I was running shit and I was going to change the fucking game.

"I'm spendin' some quality time wit' Baby this weekend, so I need ya'll niggas to hold it down and shit," I said.

"Already," Mel said as he rubbed his Rick Ross style beard. That nigga had been a Cue forever, but he had never been interested in running shit. Deniro was also a top lieutenant of the Cues, but he liked to lay low too. They were both on their way to OG status, but couldn't seem to let go. The lure of the streets was too much and both of those niggas weren't as content as my pops and Reco obviously were at home with their women. They still needed the streets and I wasn't mad at them. Shit, I was just getting started so there was no letting go for me anytime soon either.

Cane nodded in my direction with a serious look on his high yellow face.

"You know we got this nigga," he said with his mischievous gray eyes twinkling. That nigga was ready to get into some shit.

If I was the level headed one, he was the total opposite. His mother was a white chick who had left him on his pop's doorstep when he was a couple weeks old. She said that there was no way she could raise a black kid and still be accepted by her family. That shit kind of reminded me of my mom and Caruso's situation. His pop's wife Theresa raised Cane as if she was his mother because she didn't have any children of her own. She also didn't leave her husband. Cane's pops was an OG who was killed in prison when Cane was seven. That Cue life was all that he knew and although I was supposed to be shielded from it, the streets felt like an old friend to me. I guess that shit was in my blood because although I hadn't been exposed to it early on, I fell into it at the age of fifteen like I hadn't known anything else. It was like second nature to me and I finally had the family that I wanted.

"No bullshitting Cane. I need you to be on point. I don't need you to be all up in the strip clubs the whole weekend. I know how you can be 'bout some ass nigga."

Cane shook his head at me like he was disappointed in the truth. That nigga stayed fucking with hoes way more than I used to before I met Mackie. There were times when we had to go pull his drunk ass up out of the strip club. He was always trying to get some pussy by any means necessary. There was nothing wrong with that, but it was supposed to be money over bitches. How could I expect for that muthafucka to have my back if he was always fucking something or trying to fuck?

"A'ight nigga damn," Cane spat as he frowned at me. "You act like a nigga don't know how to handle shit when you gone. What the fuck man?" His thick eyebrows seemed to join as he ran his hand across his wavy hair.

"Pretty boy ass mufucka," I laughed as I shook my head. "I need you to be worried a little less about your swag gettin' you some pussy and a little bit more about gettin' that money. Focus nigga. Money, then clothes and hoes."

"What? Your pops taught you that?" Cane asked with a slight chuckle.

"Oh, okay nigga…" I started to roast that mufucka.

"Err'thang goin' be kosher nigga. Handle your business," Deniro said interrupting our bruh fight. "It's just one thing though."

"What's that?" I asked suddenly getting serious because of his tone.

"It's these niggas who say they from Macon who keep poppin' up on Glenwood and shit. Don't nobody know them niggas, but they claim that they wanna do some business. I told them niggas I don't know what the fuck they talkin' 'bout. What fuckin' business? Honestly I ain't tryin' to fuck wit' 'em, but I'll find out whatever I can. They up to something, but I can't call it yet."

"Hmm, them niggas probably on some set up shit," Mel spoke up with a blunt full of Gas dangling from his lips. He took a few puffs and passed it to Cane.

That shit seemed strange as hell. "What type of set up shit you thinkin' 'bout Mel? You think they the Feds or dope boys lookin' for a come up?" I asked.

He shrugged his shoulders. "I'on know yet nigga. It's either or."

Deniro shook his head. "I agree, but we ain't doin' no kinda business with them mufuckas."

I nodded. "Go wit' your gut. Ain't none of ya'll niggas new to this shit. If you think I need to stay and…"

"Nah. Gone handle your business wit' yo' shawty." Deniro shook his head. "You trippin' my nigga."

"For real," Cane said as he passed me the blunt. "'Cause if I had a chick who look like, what's her name?"

"Mackie," Mel spoke up all quick and shit.

That shit made my skin crawl. I just didn't like other mufuckas talking about my girl like that.

"Mackie, yeah, I'd be MIA all up in that ass," Cane laughed.

"You tryin' to catch some shots ain't you nigga? I don't play no games 'bout my girl man." My facial expression had to let that nigga know that I was dead ass.

"Yeah, that nigga don't play 'bout Baby," Deniro teased.

"Fuck ya'll. Just handle shit and hit me if you need to. I'm leavin' in the mornin'," I said as I stood up.

If I didn't get the hell out of there one of them niggas were going to end up in the ER for real.

*   *   *

"Okay, keep your eyes closed," I told Baby as I held on to her hand.

"What the hell Zy?" She asked as she let me lead the way to her surprise.

I chuckled. "No worries lil' mama. You know I ain't gon' let nothin' crazy happen to you."

"You better not," she said with a slight smile.

When we were finally at our destination I told her to open her eyes.

Her beautiful, brown eyes fluttered open and I waited for her reaction.

"For real baby?" Her eyes were wide with anticipation and excitement.

"Yup. We're goin' for a helicopter ride mama."

The dimples in her cheeks came out to play as I helped her get in.

"Where're we going?" She asked excitedly as she sat down.

I sat next to her behind the pilot and the sound of the propellers made me speak louder.

"You'll see."

She batted her sexy eyes at me. "I love surprises."

"And I love you," I said before grabbing a bottle of Moet and two champagne glasses.

My baby licked her lips and then flashed me a tantalizing smile. "I love you too, but why do I feel like you got something up your sleeve?"

I smiled back at her. "Cuz you know I'm always up to something."

"So, are you telling me that I got you all figured out already?" She poked her lips out. "That's no fun," she said as she reached for the glass I'd just filled up for her.

"Nope," I nodded. "You think you got me all figured out, but you don't. I'm always a step ahead shorty."

"Oh really?" She asked as she took a sip of the champagne. That alluring ass smile was back on her face.

There was a moment of calm as the helicopter ascended into the blue, cloudless sky.

"I'd rather show you than talk about it," I said as we clinked our glasses together.

"Hmmm, okay. I guess I'll stop asking questions and just wait and see."

"I think you should," I agreed.

We laughed, sipped some more and talked. When the helicopter finally landed behind the property at Lake Lanier her eyes were all wide and shit. There was a picnic blanket and basket set up waiting for us beside the water. I'd gone there earlier to make sure that everything was in order. Well, with the help of my pops of course, I pulled out all the stops. By Sunday Baby's doubts were going to be permanently erased and I would feel more comfortable about leaving her to handle Caruso's ass. Until then I had to make sure that my relationship was intact first. I had to know that my girl would be waiting for me with opened arms.

Baby looked like her face was going to crack she was smiling so damn hard. I loved that shit and I couldn't help but smile too. Seeing her look so happy just did something to me that I'd never felt before. It was like I had finally found my place and it was with her. A nigga had never felt so damn complete in my life. To be honest, I hadn't felt like that since before I lost my mother. To compare her presence to something so sacred let me know that she was indeed special. I felt like my mother was smiling down on me for making such a good choice.

"Wow, Zy, this is…I don't even have the words," she said as she sat down on the blanket.

"Turn your phone off," I said wiping the smile from my face. The look I was giving her was a demanding, I run shit expression. "No texting, no Instragram and no fuckin' Facebook."

"Who you think you G checkin'?" She asked giving me a serious look back.

"I need your undivided attention right now," I said as I sat next to her.

She kissed me softly on the lips. "Okay baby. You got that."

"Good." I thought about the old school R&B my pops had put on my iPod. I was wondering if I should wait until later, or just go ahead and get some of that sweet pussy right then and there.

Her lips felt so good on mine, damn. I wanted her so bad, but something told me to wait.

"Mmmm, okay baby." She pulled away from me reluctantly. "What did you prepare for us? I know you didn't cook anything."

"See, that's what I'm talkin' 'bout right there. You don't know a nigga like you think you do. Just 'cause I been takin' you out to eat don't mean I don't know how to cook ma."

She gave me a doubtful look. "You can't cook Zy. Remember when you burned the turkey bacon?"

I laughed. "That was 'cause you were distractin' me."

She giggled and then smirked at me. "How was I distracting you?"

"You didn't have nothin' on under that tee shirt and those lil' chunky ass cheeks were pokin' out. The turkey bacon burned 'cause my attention was on that ass."

She nodded in agreement. "Okay, but you have to learn to focus. Don't let a fat ass be your down fall."

"I'd fall down anywhere for your fat ass."

She busted into laughter as she opened the picnic basket. "So, I take it that you came out here to set all of this up. When did you get the chance to do that?"

"Stop tryna figure shit out. Just enjoy it. You're too analytical ma. I love that you're smart and inquisitive, but I need you to relax a little bit."

She peered up at me. "I'm relaxed and what's up with the big words."

"Not relaxed enough and just 'cause I'm a street nigga don't mean I ain't a smart nigga."

"True. You are smart baby and how relaxed do you want me to be?"

When she looked up at me with those damn eyes again, I almost lost it. Damn, what the hell had that woman done to me?

"What?" She asked as I stared at her.

"Nothin' ma. You're just so damn fine."

"You're the one that's fine," she said as she pulled the food out of the basket. "And I'm hungry."

"Chill out ma. Let me fix our plates. Damn. Can you let me cater to you?" I asked wondering why she wouldn't just let me do for her.

With a shrug, she backed down and let me take over. I put a turkey sub on her plate along with Doritos, which I knew was her favorite snack. There was also potato salad and more Moet.

"Thank you," she said when I placed her plate in front of her.

"You're welcome," I said before taking a bite of my sandwich.

We ate and talked of course. Our conversations were always so fluid and flowed like water. It was just something about her that made it so easy to express myself. Most women didn't make me feel that at ease. I'd always been comfortable around the opposite sex, because females always seemed so drawn to me, but never had I been able to be so real. Baby was something else and when I was with her all I wanted was more time. Damn, I wanted more and more of her. It wasn't just about sex either. Her sex was good, damn good, but what we had was so much deeper than that.

*   *   *

After we wrapped our picnic up, I led her to the lake house that my pops had hooked me up with. It was a modern, two story log cabin that sat right there by the water. The sun had set, so the lights around the house made it look even grander that it was.

"Oh my God. This is amazing," Mackie whispered as she took in the scenery. Her face lit up as we walked up to the front door.

"Wait until you see the inside," I said as I pulled the key out.

I pushed the door open and her astonishment showed. The place was incredible and after the tour was over, we lounged lazily on the sofa together. When I pulled a baggie of trees out of my pocket and a blunt, she wrinkled her nose up at me.

"I know you don't smoke, but you ain't gotta look like that."

"What's the big deal about weed anyway?" She asked as she watched me gut the Swisher.

"You probably need some weed," I joked. "It might help you wind down."

"So, you think I'm too uptight?" She asked sounding offended. "I guess you're used to chicks that are loose."

I shook my head. "I ain't mean it like that ma. What I'm used to don't matter, so I wish you'd stop throwin' that shit in my face. I'm wit' you and I want you to enjoy a nigga. It seem like you can't loosen up around me and I just want you to trust me. I ain't gonna hurt you Baby, but this shit here is real life. It ain't gon' be no fairytale. No relationship is. We gon' have our moments, but through it all I know that my love'll only grow for you. I just want you to let go wit' me. That's all."

"I'm not trying to throw anything in your face Zy. I just don't know how to take you. You seem so sweet and sensitive, but you're a drug dealer. Not only that, but I'm sure you…kill people. How do I know that I'm not just something…?"

"Hell nah shorty, I ain't gon' have that shit," I said shutting her ass down real quick. "You gotta be fuckin' kiddin' me right now. Did you not agree to be wit' me after already knowin' all that shit?"

I watched as she nodded with her eyes on the floor.

"You can't even look at me?" I asked. "I ain't hear your answer ma."

She looked up at me. "Yes, I can and yes I did agree to be with you after already knowing that shit."

"Why?" I asked as I sprinkled the weed in the blunt.

"Because I'm in love with you," she answered. "And I don't care about any of that as long as you're good to me."

I started rolling the blunt up and stared at her while I did it. She needed to know that she could get licked just like that mufucka if she acted right, but nah, she wanted to be questioning a nigga's intentions and shit.

"You sure?" That time when I licked the blunt I kept my eyes on her. I over exaggerated the licking motion and let her eyes linger on my tongue. "Cause you don't seem sure."

"I'm sure," she insisted breathlessly.

"I'on know ma," I said as I dried the blunt with a black Bic lighter. "I feel like you got your doubts and shit. You think a nigga tryna play your ass. If only your fine ass knew what my plans *really* are for you."

She stared up at me intensely. "What are your plans Zy?" When she let out a sarcastic laugh it surprised me. "Because I've made plans plenty of times, but nothing ever goes as planned."

I lit the blunt and took a pull before I responded. "Didn't I tell you to stop askin' questions?"

"That ain't fair." She pouted.

"Life ain't fair." I blew the smoke out of my nose.

Baby shook her head. "Let me hit that shit."

"What? You wanna hit the blunt?"

"Yeah."

"Nah."

"You can't tell me what to do!" She snapped suddenly. "I'm sick of being the good girl. Let me hit that shit."

I smiled slyly. "So, hitting this blunt's gonna make you bad huh?"

"No, but it's a step in the right direction." She smiled back at me before grabbing the blunt.

"You ever smoked weed before?" I asked curiously.

"No," she said before taking a long, hard pull.

That was a huge mistake because just as soon as she inhaled, she started coughing hard as hell.

I rubbed her back gently as I waited for her to catch her breath. "You can't hit that shit that hard ma. Slow down, damn. You said you ain't smoked before."

She cleared her throat once she finally got herself together. After that she passed the blunt back to me and shook her head.

"Fuck that. You can have that shit." She coughed to clear her lungs again.

I laughed. "You gotta take your time lil' mama. Your ass 'bout to be high as hell though."

Suddenly she started laughing hard as hell like I'd just said the funniest shit she'd ever heard. Yup, shorty was fucked up. That shit had me bugging. In no time tears were falling from her eyes as she laughed hysterically. All I could do was sit there and wait for it to pass. Usually when people smoked loud ass weed for the first time ever, they had weird reactions like laughing fits. A minute or so went by before she finally calmed down.

"Oh my God. I'm really high and I only took one damn pull. What the hell is in that shit?" She asked with her wide eyes glued to the blunt between my fingers.

I passed it back to her. "It's called THC," I laughed. "Try it again, but take your time ma. Let the smoke accumulate in your mouth and then inhale. Don't try to take all of the smoke at once. You still at amateur status and this shit here ain't no mid."

She looked at me with a quizzical expression on her face. "What's the difference?"

"I'll explain it later Baby. Let's just chill for now." I leaned over and kissed her cheek as she tried hitting the blunt again. Damn she smelled even better than that Kush that was burning.

That time she didn't choke at all and actually puffed it a few times before she passed it back. In no time the blunt was gone and Baby finally had control of her emotions. She seemed to be more in her element and was a whole lot more laid back. Hmm, she was cool as fuck when she was high. I mean, baby girl was cool as hell sober, but the weed gave her an edge. I liked it. A nigga wasn't trying to get her addicted to that shit or nothing. I'd never let her try anything else. Nah, I loved her ass too much to ruin her life. Besides, when it came to the opposite sex I was a sucker. Needless to say, the lack of a mother figure in my life had made me mad sensitive toward most females.

Next thing I knew, the weed had the effect on her that every man wanted.

"You're looking really good right now," she said sexily as she leaned over to kiss me. Her eyes were all low and shit.

"Right now?" I asked playfully. "So, I'on always look good to you?"

She smiled and kissed me again. "Mmm, you always look good baby, but right now you're looking extra fuckin' good."

"And you…"

Before I could even finish she literally had her tongue down my throat.

When she finally let a nigga come up for air I was out of breath. "Damn."

She flashed me a sexy ass look and then stood up. My eyes didn't move away from her body as she slowly removed her clothes. With only a bra and panties on, she teased me by only allowing a short peek at her breasts and then that pretty ass pussy. There was not even a smile on my face because shit was about to get real. There was a look of shock on her face when I stood and picked her up. My lips were on hers in no time and her legs were securely wrapped around my waist. Her arms were around my neck in a tight embrace, but I didn't mind. All I did was carry her sexy ass to the nearest bedroom.

"I got a special weekend planned for us, but right now all I wanna do is taste you," I whispered against her soft lips.

Then I thought about the love making music on my iPod and got up to connect it to the speakers that I'd conveniently put in the room. Music nowadays wasn't the same as what my moms used to play. I wasn't trying to eat Baby out to no rap and shit. When I pressed play the sound of Jodeci's old school slow jam "Stay" filled the romantic space around us. There were also candles all over the room that I decided to light. After I set the mood, I turned the light off and stared down at my sexy love as the flames of the candles illuminated her beautiful face.

My mouth was watering, so I hurriedly removed her panties to indulge in my favorite dessert. Baby was looking at me like her life depended on whatever I was about to do to her. The longing in her eyes made me want to please her and so I did that shit to the fullest.

"Ohhhh, Zy…" she moaned as she stared down at me with her sexy, thick lips slightly parted.

Her hair cascaded over her shoulder and if I could've captured that moment I would've. The look of ecstasy on her pretty face made me really appreciate what I had. She was the epitome of everything that I'd ever wanted and I wasn't foolish enough not to take full advantage.

"Mmm…you taste…so sweet…" I did my favorite tongue tricks and that shit had her grinding that fat, juicy pussy in circles.

"Uhhh…damn…that feels…soooo…good…mmm," she whispered with her eyes still stuck on me and what I was doing. Her hands were softly caressing my face.

I loved that shit though. It made me perform even better. Baby's pussy was so fresh and she was on her grown woman shit. Although she didn't wax it clean, the hair was trimmed really close. A nigga appreciated that shit, because it was hard to maneuver around a bush. I didn't mind, because good pussy was good pussy, but I appreciated when a woman took care of the landscape.

"Open it up," I demanded. My pointer and middle fingers were deep inside of that sopping wet pussy and my other hand was cupping that fat ass, so I was preoccupied.

She complied and used her fingers to spread her meaty folds. Damn, my girl's pussy was mad fat. I was fucked up over that shit, because contrary to belief all pussy was not the same. Hers was the best I'd ever had and although I was a young nigga I'd had enough to know what was good and what wasn't. Baby's surpassed good and that was the reason why I didn't mind sucking on that sweet ass pussy until she begged me to stop. I didn't understand how a nigga couldn't make her cum. Shit, it was my pleasure.

"I'm 'bout to cum Zy…" she expressed in a sexy voice as she grabbed my face and tried to pull me away from her swollen clitoris.

Of course I didn't let go. I grabbed her ass, locked her in place, sucked her clit like an expert and fingered that pussy until her juices were pouring down like a fountain. 'Hell yeah," I cockily thought to myself.

"Zyyyyyyyyyy….uhhhhh…fuck!" She screamed and gyrated with her face all balled up in orgasmic pleasure. I could've sworn I saw tears in her eyes.

I just continued sucking on her clit and enjoying the way her pussy muscles were contracting around my fingers. My dick was going to enjoy that shit even more, but I wanted to taste her a little bit longer. Shit, we had all of our lives to fuck. For the time being I'd just get my pleasure from pleasing her.

Her eyes looked so damn vulnerable and I knew that she was just begging for a nigga to continue being the man that she had fallen in love with. I stared into her eyes and made a silent vow to never let her down.

"I love you Baby and all I wanna do is make you feel like this. I ain't tryna hurt you." Okay, so I had to express it in words.

The tears that I saw in her eyes fell down her cheeks and I moved up to kiss them away.

"You promise?" She asked softly with her beautiful eyes still on me.

"I promise," I said staring into her eyes as I moved down to taste her love again.

Chapter 3

Mackie

I was the first one to wake up the next morning at the crack of dawn. My smile was all big when I remembered the night before. Zy's sexy ass had ate me out for hours and I came so much that it took me no time to fall asleep. He didn't even try to get some ass and that made me want to return the favor. I got out of the bed without waking him up and rushed to the bathroom. After taking a quick shower and brushing my teeth, I tiptoed back to the bed. He was still asleep. Damn, I couldn't believe that I was into a man who was younger than me. It was only by about six months because my birthday was in February and his was in August, but I normally dated guys who were older than me. I had to admit that I was glad when my mother said that she wanted to move to Atlanta. I had ignored Zy all of the times he tried to holla, but from the moment I saw his fine ass, I wanted him just as bad as he wanted me.

Men like him scared the shit out of me though. I'd always avoided the thug type because my mother told me to. Those type of men represented my father; the man who wasn't there. The thing was I didn't know if he would've been there if he was still alive. All I knew was that his lifestyle took him away from me. That made me feel like I wanted to be with a man who avoided life threatening situations, but honestly anything could happen to anybody. A straight laced business man could get killed in a car accident on his way to work. Being with Zy in such a small amount of time had already made me want to love with no boundaries. He wasn't my father and I wasn't my mother. We had our own fate; our own destiny and I was ready to sit back and let it unfold. Well, at least at that moment I did.

I climbed on the bed and Zy was still asleep. That was good because I wanted him to wake up to me serving him early in the AM. My man needed to know that although I had my doubts about us being together, I knew for a fact that I loved the shit out of his ass. Honestly I wanted us to work more than anything, but I also knew that the odds were against us. The streets only resulted in one or two things if not both; jail or the grave. I didn't want either of them for him. All I wanted was to know that he would be safe in my arms forever, but not knowing that would happen for a fact had me scared shitless.

For the moment I removed all of the doubts from my mind and eased over to my man. He was mine and I was going to do all I could to make sure that I kept it that way for as long as possible. Damn, he was too sexy to resist and I had to just stop trying because I wasn't winning the fight at all. He was lying on his back in just his boxers, so it was easy access to his magic wand. I liked to say that instead of dick, because I'd had a dick before. What he had was magic because he did things to my body with it that were unimaginable.

I just stared at his smooth, coffee brown skin tone as I traced my fingers down his chest to his six pack. Mmm, he was so damn enticing. There was some magnetic force that drew me to him and I couldn't defy that shit if I tried. Believe me, I had tried.

He stirred and then his light brown, bedroom eyes fluttered open. His fingers were in my hair as I teased the head of his dick with my tongue. When I took all of his morning wood in my mouth he let out a low moan.

"Mmmm..."

Yeah, I was feeling myself as I did what came naturally. I was no pro at giving head. I'd only tried it a few times with my ex, but Zy brought out the freak in me. The songs he'd played the night before were still going on and on in my head. I especially loved Jodeci because that old school R&B was that real love making music. I liked some of the new stuff that was out, but it wasn't something that I wanted to hear to set the mood right. My man was like an old soul although he was into that street life, so that made him irresistible to me. I guess you could say that I was kind of an old soul too.

I watched him and admired his facial features. His angular nose, thick, dark lips, thin moustache and trimmed beard were all a nice view from my angle. His eyes narrowed into slits and he bit his bottom lip as he stared down at me. I slurped and sucked until he lifted his torso from the bed and tried to assault my mouth with his thick, nine inches. It didn't deter me though. I was going to make him cum if it was the last thing I did. His eyes begged for mercy, but payback was a bitch. He didn't have any for me the night before, so I had none for him.

"Damn Baby, suck that shit…ahhhh," he groaned as he grabbed my head.

There were tears in my eyes and I was gagging and the whole nine, but I loved the fact that he was losing it over that shit.

His body jerked and that was a sign that he was about to bust. I really got into it then and took his full length all the way down my throat. As I did that, I hummed on it and that nigga went bananas.

"Mmmm…Baby…oh my fuckin'…mmm. Damn, you look so good ma. I'm 'bout to cum…right…fuckin'…now lookin' at your pretty ass wit' all that dick down your throat!" He started fucking my face again and then his body stiffened. "Fuck yeah…argggggghhhhhhh…shiiiiiiiiiiiitttt! I'm cumin!"

I guess it was a first time for everything, because I let him cum in my mouth. The taste was both bitter and sweet and it was definitely not something I wanted to swallow. When his body finally stopped convulsing and I knew that he was done, I quickly removed him from my mouth and sashayed to the restroom. I spit in the toilet, flushed, gargled with mouth wash, rinsed with water and returned to the bed. His eyes were closed and his dick was resting on his thigh.

"Damn ma. I wouldn't mind wakin' up to that shit more often," he said with a smile.

His eyes were slightly opened and I could tell that nut had wiped him out a little.

I snuggled up next to him. "Don't get spoiled daddy."

"Hmm, why not?"

"Because if you expect head every morning I got news for you; it ain't gon' happen."

"I'll eat your pussy every mornin' wit' no problem."

"That's cool if that's what you wanna do, but I won't press the issue," I said as I kissed his lips with his morning breath and all. For some reason his breath smelled fine. It made me wonder if he had snuck and brushed his teeth before I woke up.

"Hmm, touch it," he said in a raspy voice.

"What?" I asked knowing damn well what he was talking about.

He grabbed my hand and put it on his dick, which was hard again all of a sudden.

"Your voice does that to me." His hand traveled down south and his fingers were exploring my wetness in seconds.

"I guess you want some now," I whispered sexily as I spread my legs wider.

His eyes were open as he climbed on top of me. "I damn sure do. Don't start nothin' you can't finish shorty. You gon' learn. You know that pussy is always the best in the morning."

"Mmm, my pussy is grade A all day," I said as he slid inside of me and filled me up. "Mmm." Damn, that man's dick had me gone.

"Shit, your pussy's so fuckin' warm…tight…and wet…mmm."

Our lips joined and our tongues intertwined as our bodies became one.

"Ohhhh Zy…."

"Damn Baby…"

*   *   *

The rest of our day was filled with things to do. I had never been on a jet ski before, but that shit was fun as hell. Well, of course my bae was driving it and I was just holding on. It was like a motorcycle on the water, so I was on that shit hard. After that we rode on a speed boat and smoked a blunt. Bae claimed to know the white dude who was driving, so it was all good.

"We're going to a party after this," he said with a Corona in his hand.

I was enjoying the beautiful, sunny day and the serenity of the water surrounding me.

"A party?" I asked not really knowing if I was in the mood for that. For some reason I just wanted to lay under him.

"Yeah, what, you don't wanna go?" He asked as he removed the dark Ray Bann's that he was wearing from his handsome face.

"I don't know." I sighed. "Maybe I just want you all to myself."

He grinned sexily. "I mean, if that's what you want just say it, but I thought you'd want to get out a lil' bit."

"Well, I guess a party won't be so bad." I sipped on a sweet, mixed drink I didn't know the name of and took the blunt when he passed it to me like I'd been smoking weed forever.

He kissed my neck and whispered in my ear. "We gon' grind a lil' bit and then take it back to the spot."

My body overheated instantly and I closed my eyes against the bright, orange sun. "Okay," I whispered.

"You love me right?" He asked with his warm hands roaming inside of my tank top.

"Mmm hmm," I moaned seductively.

"You trust me?"

My eyes opened and his were on mine.

I nodded against my will. "Yes."

He kissed me deeply as I questioned my answer. Did I really trust him? Shit, I didn't know if I did or not. I had said that I did, but I was still confused. In my heart I didn't want to hurt him by making him think that I still had doubts. As much as I tried to push them into the back of my mind, or act like they didn't exist, they crept back up. It wasn't really insecurity that kept me from letting go with him. It was fear; a feeling that I couldn't shake no matter how hard I wanted to.

* * *

When we got back to the spot I went into the bedroom to prepare to get dressed. It was a good thing he'd told me to pack a bag for a couple days, but I didn't think I had anything appropriate for a fancy party. Just when I was about to turn around to tell him that I needed to get an outfit, I saw that he had a box in his hand.

"This is for you," he said before I could even speak. There was a sly grin on his face. "Yanna picked it out. I figured you'd be like most females when it comes to wantin' something new to wear to a party."

I grinned too as I looked up at him. "You were right about that."

After I carefully opened the box I pulled out a short, white Chanel dress. It was so pretty and lacey and I loved how the top of it looked like a corset.

"This is so pretty," I gasped as I looked at the size.

"I thought so too. A little too short, but pretty." He smiled.

"It's not too short." I thought about the shoes that I had with me and as if he read my mind again, he pointed at the bed.

"Shoes are in that box."

I turned around and noticed a shoe box sitting at the foot of the bed. I walked over to open it and there was a pair of red Christian Louboutin red bottom pumps. The heels were like six inches high and although I wasn't used to rocking a heel that high, I was damn sure going to try. Those shoes were hot as fuck. I pictured how I would look in the ensemble and smiled. I did have some accessories to accent the red shoes. The red and white was going to be so hot together.

"Thank you baby," I said as I turned around to give him a grateful hug.

"Now go get dressed. I know it's gonna take you forever so I'll let you have the bathroom first. I'm just gonna chill and make a few phone calls," he said before giving me a kiss.

"Phone calls?" I gave him the side eye. "Why would you be making phone calls right now? I thought this was our time."

He kissed me again. "This is our time ma. I just need to hit my pops up and then call Cane to check on some shit. Don't worry. You'll have my undivided attention for the rest of the time we're here."

I nodded in satisfaction as I stood on my tip toes to kiss him more passionately that time. There was a feeling that I just couldn't shake though and it wasn't a good one. My instinct told me to hold on to the moment before us, because our time together would be cut short. I didn't know how it was going to happen, when or why, but I just knew that we weren't going to always be as happy as we were right then. Something was bound to happen and it was going to test our love for sure. Damn, I didn't want to feel that way, but my intuition had never lied to me before.

After I broke our kiss, I turned to go into the bathroom without lingering to stare into his sexy, light brown eyes for too long. I didn't want him to know what I was thinking. One thing I did notice about Zy was his ability to read me so easily. If he looked into my eyes he'd know that his attempt at a romantic weekend hadn't worked at erasing any of the doubts that I had. What he wouldn't understand was the fact that my doubts were not in him or his love for me. I just knew that our relationship had no chance of working from the start and that was the reason I'd tried to avoid falling for him in the first place.

*   *   *

Zyon

I was wrapping up my phone call with that nigga Cane when Baby walked into the room.

"Damn," I gasped with my mouth hanging open. "Wow. You look…damn…I don't even have words for how you look right now Baby. I'll hit you up later nigga."

"A'ight," Cane said before I hung up the phone.

After that I let it fall to the sofa's cushion and stood up to greet my gorgeous girlfriend with a kiss. My dick was hard as hell at the sight of her soft curves in all white. She looked like a sexy ass angel and I wanted to undress her and take my time making love to her fine ass. I knew that I'd said we were going to a party, so I had to dismiss the thought of getting up in it until later.

"Mmm, thank you baby," she said when I pulled away from her. "Is everything good?"

"Yeah, everything's good lil' mama. Especially the way that dress is fittin' you. Damn!" I had to adjust my hardness and shit as I stared at her smooth, mocha complexion.

I just loved her body. She wasn't super thick, but she was thick in all the right places. Her waist was slim and I loved the slope of her nice hips and juicy little ass. She even had the perfect sized breasts to complete a sexy little package. Yeah, I was in love like a muthafucka for real.

It was like she was glowing as she smiled up at me. She was pure gorgeous and I loved how she accentuated the white dress with a slim, red leather belt and pretty ruby studs in her ear. The way she didn't over do it and kept the accessories simple was a plus. I liked how she didn't look like a chicken head when she put her outfits together. My baby girl was classy and that was what attracted me to her the most.

She had her hair pinned up on the sides, which showed off her pretty face. Her cheekbones were supermodel high and the blush she'd put on made them show more than usual. The nude lipstick and neutral colored eye shadow were not too much makeup, but it was enough to make her look more grown up. Her almond shaped, dark brown eyes were full of passion as she stared into my eyes lustfully.

"You like it baby?" She spun around and then did a sexy pose for me.

I turned to grab my phone. "Stay just like that sexy."

When I turned she was flashing me a sultry smile. "Perfect," I said as I snapped a couple pictures of her.

"Thank you Zy," she said softly as she kissed my cheek.

"After a while you're gonna get so used to this kinda treatment that you'll stop thankin' me."

She laughed. "I don't think I'll ever stop thanking you."

I reluctantly pulled away from her. "I'm gonna go get ready and then we'll be out okay."

"I'm in no hurry baby," she said as she stood there still looking all enticing and shit.

"Mmm, it's so hard to walk away from you when you lookin' like that," I said with my eyes glued to her as I left the room.

She gave me a teasing wave as I disappeared into the bedroom. I grabbed a white and black Givenchy print tee shirt, a pair of black and white True Religion fatigue shorts and my low top white and black Air Ones. After brushing my teeth and a quick shower I sprayed on some Gucci cologne and got dressed. Then I slid on a thin, short platinum rope chain and my platinum Rolex before putting a white and black A fitted on my head. Simple, but still swagged out.

I joined my lady in the sitting room and grabbed her hand. "You ready?" I asked as she picked up a small red clutch bag from the sofa.

"Yes," she said in a sweet voice that made my body over heat.

I had a feeling that we were not going to be at that party for long.

"Hold up babe," I said stopping her in her tracks.

As I held my phone up to take a selfie of us, I kissed her cheek lovingly. It was a good thing I thought about leaving my car there right before the helicopter ride. Before we made it to my Charger I posted the pic on Instagram and Facebook with the hashtags #MeandBaby #LoveHerLife. That was for Kia's spiteful ass. A dose of her own medicine would do her trifling ass some good.

*　　*　　*

About an hour or so had passed and we were having a good time dancing and getting fucked up. The party was at my nigga Duke's crib. He was also a Cue who had a nice crib on the Lake. There were plenty of drinks, food, and drugs to indulge in. The only thing I was interested in doing was blowing some loud and getting my drink on. There were mufuckas popping Mollys, drinking Lean and sniffing that powder. Some of the chicks were practically naked or coming out of their clothes. The music was pumping and there were a few partiers who were acting like they wanted to fuck right there on the dance floor. I watched as Baby's eyes widened at how turnt up those niggas were acting in that joint.

"I feel a little over dressed," she said playfully as I possessively kept her close to me.

I laughed. "No you ain't ma. There ain't no way I'd let you go out of the house lookin' like half of these chicks in here."

"I thought this was going to be a classy, fancy party. I mean, look at this dress." She scanned the room with a look of disdain on her face.

"Well, I want you to look classy no matter where we go. I take it that this ain't your crowd." As I looked around the room I noticed that many of the people there were decked out in the latest, most expensive gear, but that was mostly the men.

For some reason I noticed that when I went out women seemed really thirsty lately. The outfits were getting skimpier and less tasteful as time went on. I was a man and I did appreciate a sexy woman, but it was a time and a place for everything. If I wanted to see butt naked ass I would go to a strip club.

"It's not really that. It's not like I think I'm too good or I'm better than anybody. It's just that if something pops off I won't be able to run in these high ass heels." She laughed and then kissed my neck softly.

"Hmm, you ain't gotta worry 'bout runnin' lil' ma. I'll carry your fine ass to the car and strap you in and everything. I'm that nigga that's gon' be gunnin' at niggas to make sure you good. No worries when you wit' me. I'm gon' always protect you Baby. Know that."

She nodded. "And I believe you."

"You should. You hungry babe? We been grindin' and smokin' and shit. I know you got the munchies ma, 'cuz I do."

"Yeah, I can eat something," she said.

"I'll grab something. You stay right here. I'll be back."

I leaned over and kissed my second favorite set of lips before I got up.

On my way to where the buffet was set up, I ran into my boy Duke. He was a tall, built dark skinned cat with shoulder length locks. He was in his early twenties and was a lady's man for real. That nigga had three chicks hanging on to him like he was Floyd Mayweather or some shit.

"Zy, what's up man?" He asked as he walked over to give me a gangsta hug.

"Ain't shit Duke."

"LeAnne, Christy and Milan, meet my nigga Zy. He runnin' shit like his old man Diablo, the legend."

All three of the women smiled at me. They were bad as hell, but I wasn't interested.

"Hi," one of them said sexily. She looked like she was Asian and black and her body was stacked like a platter of pancakes.

I only nodded and then my attention went back to Duke. "A'ight my nigga. I'm 'bout to go grab

something for me and my girl to eat on. Thanks for invitin'
us man. This shit is tight."

Duke smiled and glanced at his girls before
looking back at me. I guess that was his way of asking if I
was sure I didn't want to borrow one of them for the night.

"A'ight man. Do you and I'm gon' do me.
Tell your pops I thought he was comin'. I guess married
life got him on lock and shit."

I laughed. "You know how Yanna is. She
would've came and turned this shit out by now."

"Hmm, you might be right about that. That
nigga good where he at then. Queen don't play 'bout her
man. That's for sure," Duke chuckled good-naturedly.
"A'ight man. Holla at me before you leave."

"Will do my nigga."

I walked off in the pursuit of food and
hoped that nobody else would stop me. Shit, I had to get
back to Baby before the vultures swarmed. After putting all
of the hot wings and French fries that I could on a plate, I
walked back to my lady. There was some tall, brown
skinned dude standing next to her. That nigga was a little
too close and I could tell that she was uncomfortable. I
hadn't seen him before and I knew for a fact that he wasn't

a Cue. I didn't know who homeboy was, but he was going to catch it for fucking with my girl.

As I got closer Baby's eyes caught mine and a look of relief washed over her face. I guess she hadn't walked off because I told her to stay there. She didn't have to worry. I was going to get that nigga away from her pronto.

"You a'ight Baby?" I asked as I glared at dude.

"Yeah, I'm good," she said not taking her eyes off me.

He didn't seem to give a damn that I had just referred to her as baby. I guess in his eyes that was a generic term. Maybe he thought I was just putting in my bid like him. As I passed her the plate, I had to let that nigga know what was up.

"Uh, what's goin' on Playboy?" I asked him.

He simply nodded in my direction, but didn't seem to get the hint. "Ain't nothin'. Just talkin' to shawty and shit."

That nigga said that shit like that was supposed to be my clue to walk off or something. What the hell? That fuck nigga was about to get his teeth knocked down his throat.

I had to laugh to keep myself from beating him down right then and there. It was my dude Duke's party and I was trying to keep it peaceful. Not only that, but I didn't really want no beef around my girl. I didn't want her to have to see that side of me so soon, but that nigga was giving me no choice.

"Look man, I'm gon' give you the benefit of the doubt 'cuz you ain't know, but this *my* girl right here. The conversation you was tryna have wit' her is over nigga. So, now that you know, I expect for you to walk on off and shit, 'cuz you don't want no problems." My facial expression had to communicate the fact that he didn't want to push my buttons. Fucking with my woman was no doubt the number one way to get me heated and ready to bust my gun.

Dude glanced at me like I was just talking to hear my voice and shit. It was like it didn't even matter that I had just warned his ass. He was acting like my woman was fair game to his ass and shit. Like I hadn't just been a man about it with the peaceful way I'd let him know that she was off limits to him and his fucking conversation. A nigga like me didn't do much talking and explaining. To say that I was a man of action was the best way to describe me.

"The lady ain't said shit…"

Before he could finish whatever lame bullshit he was about to say, I landed a nice uppercut that split his lip and stained his teeth with blood. His balance faltered and he looked at me like he couldn't believe that I had punched his ass.

"Yeah nigga, she ain't gotta say shit! I said all that needed to be said! Now if you don't know who the fuck I am I'm gon' tell you one mufuckin' time! My name is Zy nigga and I run shit! Remember that shit mufucka, 'cuz if I catch you 'round my lady again I ain't gon' hit your ass wit' my fuckin' fist! You gon' catch some shots to your dome nigga!"

"Oh…shit! Hold up…Zy man, shit, that's my cousin Ro yo'. Calm down," I heard Duke say as he came up behind me. "He ain't from the A, so he don't know what's what man."

I turned around to face that nigga. "I don't give a fuck who that muthafucka is nigga. If you want your cousin to keep breathin' you'll let him know what's up."

Duke walked over to his cousin and pushed his hand into his chest to stop that nigga from making the biggest mistake of his life. He didn't want to come for me. Not at all. The end result was not going to be good for him. I didn't give a shit who his family was.

"That nigga punched me in my mouth man," Ro said with blood dripping down his chin onto his white button down shirt.

At that point everybody's attention was on us and the scene that had unfolded.

"Shit, LeAnne, go get something to wipe this nigga's mouth and shit," Duke told one of his chicks. "Ro, man, calm the fuck down man. That nigga run shit and his pops..."

"Fuck that nigga and his pops! Let me go so I can kill that nigga!" Ro yelled trying to be hard all of a sudden.

That mufucka had the chance to hit me back, but he didn't. Now that his cousin had came over he wanted to break bad and shit. I hated lame, fronting ass niggas. He was going to let his reckless ass mouth get him merked. Trying to flex and shit.

"Let's just go baby," Mackie finally spoke up with tears in her eyes. "This is getting out of hand." She put the plate down on a table nearby.

I looked at her and shook my head. "Only because of you I'm gon' walk away from this lame ass mufucka. Control your fam Duke. I'll kill that nigga and you know that's real shit."

Without saying another word, I grabbed Baby's hand and we walked out.

"You didn't have to hit him and then threaten to kill him," she said in a soft voice.

I shook my head because I knew that she wouldn't understand. "I did have to hit that nigga. If you was a man you'd understand that."

She looked up at me and I could tell that she was pissed. "The whole time I was thinking I'd have to run if something happened and you're the one who started some shit."

"I started it? What? Me protectin' you is startin' some shit?" I couldn't believe she'd just said that.

"He hadn't done anything but try to talk to me. He didn't even touch me. I told him that I was with my boyfriend, which should've been enough. Still, you could've just walked away. It didn't have to come to that," she argued as her heels clicked on the road.

I snatched the car door open and waited for her to get in. I was pissed off as I walked around to get in the driver's seat. Why the hell was she mad at me for fighting for her honor? That nigga had not only disrespected me, but he'd disrespected her too.

"I ain't talkin' bout that shit nomore. You can feel how you wanna feel about it, but as long as we're together there ain't one nigga I'm gon' let disrespect you or me. That's all the fuck I gotta say."

She didn't say anything, but I could sense her attitude. That was our first disagreement and I didn't want to argue with her. That weekend was supposed to be romantic, but instead it had made a turn for the worse. As I drove back to the spot in silence I tried to come up with a way to make it right with her. I couldn't have her mad at me, so I had to do something to fix that shit.

Chapter 4

Mackie

Richmond, VA

2001

I hated Mr. Owen. He was the ugly, fat, light skinned man with the big lips from Child Protective Services who had taken me from the only home that I knew. Just because the neighbors had called and said that my mother was unfit they came and tore my whole world apart. It was true, my mom had left me home alone a few times, but it was only for a few hours. Besides, I was more mature than the average nine year old, so I knew how to take care of myself. Yeah, she sold marijuana, but all of the people who came to cop from her were like my family. I knew most of them as my aunts and uncles, so I thought everything was all good. I had never been abused or mistreated in my life, so why the hell did I have to live with strangers?

The first night that I fell asleep in my temporary home was when my life changed for good. After that things would never be the same for me. Trust was something I'd never experience again. The pressure of something around my neck roused me from an already restless sleep. When I reached up to feel what was cutting off my breathing, my eyes instantly opened. My fifteen year old foster sister Nina was standing over me with a leather belt around my neck. She was very pretty with long, fine hair, caramel skin tone, and short petite frame. The thing was the bitch was mean as fire.

"I'm just lettin' you know right now lil' bitch, he's mine," she whispered menacingly in my ear.

I had absolutely no clue what she meant by that, so I only nodded so she'd loosen the belt from my neck so I could breath.

"Okay," I whispered back as I tried my best to get some air to my deprived lungs.

It took me some time, but I eventually found out what my foster sister's animosity was all about. There were three foster children in our home and the only other one was a boy. When Mr. Lewis snuck into my room after I'd been there for two months, everything that I was oblivious to became all too clear. He was a big, tall, intimidating dark skinned man with large hands. At first I thought he was nice looking, but he eventually started looking like a monster to me.

"Relax sweetie," he said in a soft voice as he slid his hand inside of my Mickey Mouse pajama pants.

"If you tell it they won't believe you. If your own mama don't want you who gon' believe you."

Relax my ass. I was only nine years old. My first instinct was to fight for my life, but when I tried to scream he only held me down and put his hand over my mouth to muffle the sound. When he jammed his fingers inside of my tightness I couldn't contain my tears. I hated what he was doing to me and I didn't understand why Nina seemed to like it. Mr. Lewis had a wife, but I had to endure Nina's abuse because she claimed him as her man. I instantly knew that he was doing the same thing to her, but she was in love with him. I was not. I hated him for violating me.

After that I was claustrophobic and afraid of men period. Nina was relentless when it came to her dominance in the household. She would snap on me instantly when Mrs. Lewis wasn't around. I was so afraid of her that I would lie about where my black eyes and bruises came from. I had beef over a man at the age of nine. Never in my life had I been through anything like what I was going through then. Being with my mother was a much safer environment. I cried so much because I didn't understand why they would take me away from her and put me in a home where I was being physically, sexually and mentally abused. My mother and her friends only protected me. They would never hurt me.

Six months later I got the news that I would be returning to my mother. I was so glad to hear that.

"The courts have decided that your mother is fit for you to go back home to her. We've been keeping an eye on her and she has a job now and a better place for you to live. Are you ready to go home?" Mr. Owen asked with a smile on his chubby face.

"Yes. Thank you so much Mr. Owen," I said smiling for the first time since I'd been separated from my mother. Suddenly he had become my best friend.

I never told anybody about what had happened. Not even my mother. I knew that she would want to hurt Mr. Lewis and Nina just as much as I did. In the back of my mind those memories lingered, but I always smiled and pretended that everything was okay. Now the past was affecting me and I was paying for the fact that I'd never dealt with what happened to me. The man who'd molested me and the girl who'd beat me up almost every day for a year had never paid for their crimes against me…but they would in due time. I was going to make sure of that.

*   *   *

2011

Lake Lanier, GA

The night of our little argument at the party, Zy and I didn't talk much. All I did was tell him that I'd prefer that he slept somewhere else.

"Why Baby?" He asked like he didn't understand why I was mad.

"Because what happened tonight is exactly why I don't deal with guys like you! You don't know when to just let shit go! It wasn't that serious Zy! You just wanted to look all hard and shit like that would make me see you as my fuckin' hero! I don't need you to save me! I'm not that chick and you know that! If my life was in jeopardy that would've been a totally different story! If you had punched the mufucka who molested me when I was nine I would understand that shit, but you didn't have to do that to a man who didn't even know that I was your girl."

Hot tears burned my eyes and I swiped them away before they could fall.

"What the fuck? Who fuckin' molested you?" Zy asked angrily. Obviously he had just dismissed everything I'd said except for that.

I tried to hold back the tears as I told him all about Mr. Lewis and Nina. The abuse I'd endured at their hands was fucking with me a lot more than usual. Lately I was even having reoccurring nightmares about it. Zy was the only person that I had told and it felt good to finally let it out. He held me close to him and wiped my tears away as he kissed my cheek.

"I wanted to hurt them both Zy, but I couldn't do shit. I was only nine," I sobbed and held on to him for dear life.

"I know Baby," he whispered soothingly in my ear. "I know exactly how you must've felt. The thing is I'm who the fuck I am and you love me anyway. It don't matter that you don't usually fuck wit' niggas like me. You can't control who you fell in love wit' and neither can I. If you was meant to be wit' somebody else you wouldn't be here wit' me right now. Fuck all of that shit you was programmed to think. I'm not out to hurt you, or fuck you over ma. All I wanna do is love you and protect you. I will *always* protect you, 'cause that's my instinct. I hit that nigga because he disrespected me *after* I told him that you were my woman. He disrespected you after you told him that you was wit' your man before that. If I was just tryna be a hard nigga for show, I would've punched his ass no questions asked. I know that you don't need to be saved, but I wanna save you any fuckin' way. That shit could've been worse ma, but I was more concerned about you feelin' the way you do right now." He grabbed my hand and kissed it. "I love you more than anything and I'm so fuckin' glad that I met you Mackie. For real. I won't change overnight and I can't promise you that I will even try, because whether you like it or not, you love me just the way I am. All I know is that I want to make you happy and if that means that I have to hold that street shit at bay sometimes then so be it." He gave me an intense look as he stared down at me. "But, I promise you that I will kill the mufucka who hurt you. All I need is a name and that nigga will burn like he fuckin' deserves."

Damn, I could tell that he was mad beyond anything I could have ever felt for Mr. Lewis. As I caressed his face softly, the beast inside of him seemed to calm down a little.

I sighed. "His name is Roderick Lewis and he lived in Richmond the last time I checked. I found him and Nina on Facebook a few months ago. His old perverted ass is still married and is probably still messing with young girls. The internet has made it even easier and I know that he's hurt someone else. He must be stopped."

Zy nodded. "I'll take care of that nigga. Don't you worry. If you want, I'll handle that bitch too. I don't give a fuck."

I sighed as he pulled me into his hard chest for a tight embrace. Damn, as mad as I was at him, I felt so damn loved. "Thank you baby," I whispered knowing that I would never be content with life until I knew that Nina and Mr. Lewis had received their due karma for damaging me. "But let me think about it okay. I don't really know what I want to do right now and I want to make sure that I can live with whatever decision I make. Don't do anything until I give you the word."

"Okay," he agreed and then kissed my lips softly. "But just know that I got you. So, do you forgive me for last night? I mean, you gotta understand that what I did was outta love. It's hard to explain, but I'm a man. I'm never gonna think like you want me to, because you're a woman. Let's just agree to disagree and love each other."

"I forgive you babe, but you can't fight every man who tries to talk to me. In that case you're gonna be fighting all the time, because I'm fine as hell." I laughed as he grabbed me and held on to me tighter than before.

"That's the problem right there. You're so damn fine." He covered my face with kisses before planting a passionate one on my lips.

"I love you Zy,"

"And I love you too Baby. With whatever heart I got left."

*   *   *

I was at Princess and Tre's spot chilling in front of the television and texting Zy the next evening. Our romantic rendezvous was over and I was pissed because his ex Kia just had to comment on the pictures he'd posted of us on Instagram and Facebook.

Me: I'm sick of that bitch.

Zy: I no Baby, but fuck her. I blocked her ass. Let the haters hate.

Me: That's easy for u to say cuz u ain't gotta deal wit my ex.

Zy: Why won't u just talk to me Baby?

Me: Cuz I don't feel like talkin right now. I'm pissed.

That heifer had the nerve to like the pictures and then posted, "Oh, how cute. Now let's see how long that bullshit lasts."

Zy: I know, but don't let her do this.

Me: What?

Zy: Have us beefin' and shit to the point where u don't feel like talkin to a nigga.

Me: I'll call u later. I'm bout to watch a movie.

Zy: Wow. Really? U dismissin me for a fuckin' movie?

Me: Honestly I'd rather watch drama on TV than live it.

Zy: Ok then ma. Hit me up after your movie. Smh

Me: What u shakin ur head for?

Zy: Fuck it. Dat shit don't matter.

Me: Well fuck it then. U give up 2 easily.

Zy: Cuz I don't know how to get thru to u.

Me: Don't even try then. It ain't worth it right?

Zy: It's more than worth it, but ur ass wanna be fuckin actin all childish and shit.

Me: Childish? Whatever nigga. I'll ttyl.

He didn't respond and I didn't give a fuck. After sitting there not able to concentrate on the movie, I decided to lie down and try to take a nap. I wanted to put my hands on Kia, but I didn't know the first place to find that bitch. My frustration made it hard to rest, so I sat up and started flipping through the channels again. The house was quiet because Princess and the twins were at her mother's house and Tre was upstairs working in his study. When the doorbell rang it surprised me. I figured that it was someone there to check up on Tre, so I got up to answer the door although I didn't feel like it.

To my shock Zyon was standing there with an apologetic expression on his face. The sudden urge to forgive him right away washed over me, but I pretended to really be annoyed by his pop up visit.

"What are you doing here?" I asked heatedly as I stepped out and closed the door behind me.

"You wouldn't talk to me on the phone, so I came by to see if you'd talk to me face to face," he said with his eyes pleading for me.

I had to look away because the look he kept flashing at me was working. Why wouldn't he just give up and let me be? There was no way either of us could be ready for what the future could possibly bring. I was trying to prepare myself for school in a whole new city and I didn't have time to be fussing with some chicken head over him. Then on top of all of that my mother would be back in a few days and I already knew that she was going to give me hell about being with a street nigga. At first I wanted to work it out and defy all odds, but I had to put my energy into what was important. At that point it seemed that a relationship with him was not something that I wanted at the top of my priority list. I had to tell him that.

"I don't think the two of us being together right now is a good idea Zy. At first I did and I honestly do love you. It's just that things are starting off a little too dramatic for me. Things with Kia are just going to get worse and I know that my mom isn't going to approve. It's no point in either of us putting ourselves in the position to get hurt or to be…"

"And you said I give it up easily," Zy cut me off as he shook his head.

The look on his face at that point showed that he was agitated.

"Well, sometimes some things just ain't worth fighting for." My eyes stung as I said that and the lump in my throat seemed to be getting bigger.

He stared into my eyes in disbelief and I didn't break our eye contact. "You don't mean that shit."

I nodded. "Yes I do. I don't want to be with you Zy."

"You don't want to be wit' me, but you love me though. How much sense does that make?" He looked confused as he kept his eyes on mine.

I had to look away that time. "It makes perfect sense. Just because we love each other doesn't mean that we have to be together. Think about it Zy. I have to start at a new school in a couple months and I don't need to be distracted. We had some great moments and we shared things that we've never told anyone else, but you don't have to worry. All of your secrets are safe with me and I hope mine are safe with you. I just know that if we stay together it's going to be passion and love there, but it's going to always be some drama and I need to focus right now. I hope you understand."

He grunted before responding and it was obvious that his frustration with me was growing into anger. "Fuck that bullshit Mackie. How can a woman who claims she's so strong be such a fuckin' coward? Your ass is so afraid of feelin' something for me, so you let every little small thing make you wanna give up and shit. What we got *is* worth fightin' for, but I can't be fightin' for it by myself. Shit, you could try to meet a nigga half way, but you don't want to. Kia's just some jealous chick from my past who's scorned and you just gon' let her scare you away. Well, you know what Mackie, fuck it then. If you don't want to be wit' me, then I'll give you exactly what the fuck you want. Let Kia know that she won when you get the chance ma."

I just stood there looking stupid as hell as he turned on his heels and walked away. Something told me to follow him, but I had too much pride. Shit, I was the one who had broken it off with him first. He just agreed to it. I didn't think he would though. Deep down inside I wanted him to fight a little harder, but maybe he was right. I was a coward and I couldn't handle what came with being with a man like him. So, instead of going behind him, I opened the door and walked back inside. As the tears slid down my face, I plopped down on the sofa and cried my eyes out.

* * *

Zyon

"What ya'll niggas find out about those mufuckas from Macon?" I asked as I took a huge gulp of my Bud Light.

We were at Magic City chilling in the VIP with bottles and good green on deck. None of us were indulging in any lap dances or anything just yet. Instead we were catching up on some shit. A nigga was trying my hardest to get my mind off what had happened with Mackie, so I thought some naked hoes would be a welcome distraction from the streets and my relationship drama.

Mel spoke up first. "Not shit. They ain't been around lately and don't none of the niggas we fuck wit' in Macon know 'em like that. They said the names sound familiar, so they gon' ask around and shit."

"Yeah," Deniro said. "They ain't been back on the block, so right now we don't know what them niggas tryna do. I just let them niggas know to keep they eyes and ears open for suspicious shit. One wrong miscalculated step can result in some real shit. I'm waitin' cause I got a feelin' that shit's too quiet right now cause it's the calm before the fuckin' storm. Some crazy shit 'bout to go down and right now we just don't know what the fuck it is."

"What was those niggas' names again?" I asked.

"Dub and Ceelo, or some bullshit like that," Cane said with his eyes glued to this thick dancer named Unique's ass as she made each cheek twerk one by one and then at the same time. "Damn that bitch Unique is bad as fuck!"

Damn, I knew that trying to discuss business in a strip club was a bad idea when it came to a nigga like Cane. Unique *was* bad though. That nigga wasn't lying about that shit. She was an almond complexioned, statuesque beauty with long, straight weave down her back, the signature huge stripper ass and small waist. At about 5'11 in her six inch stilettos, she was thick and knew how to work that body. As she climbed the pole to the top, spread her legs wide open and slid down before flipping over to do a split, dollars went flying on stage. Niggas were trampling each other to get to her fine, flexible ass.

That short distraction almost kept me from seeing some shit that was unfolding right to the left of me. As the strobe lights flashed multiple colors all over the dimly lit club, I saw the chrome barrel of a hand gun in my peripheral vision. I quickly reached in my pocket and pulled out my black 380 special and pressed it in that nigga's rib cage just as he got close enough to me. Before he could press the trigger of his gun, I let off six rounds. That shit was so quick.

Pow! Pow! Pow! Pow! Pow! Pow!

Blood was everywhere. It gushed all over the table, chairs and bottles of premium alcohol. The crazy thing was not much of it had hit me because of where he was standing.

The crowd dispersed in a panic before that mufucka's body could even hit the floor. Strippers were running outside butt naked and it looked like a stampede of horses with their big asses jumping. Me and my niggas were right behind the pandemonium like I wasn't involved in the shooting. Without saying a word we got in our individual vehicles and peeled off. I would explain to them later that the nigga who had pulled out and attempted to murder me in a crowded club was Duke's cousin who had tried my girl at that party.

It was a good thing I'd thought to bring my 380 because that muthafucka could be easily hidden in my hand. When security was frisking me at the door, I just held that shit up with my palm closed around it. They didn't see it because it was black and it was dimly lit at the entrance of the club. There were no metal detectors to walk through or hand wands, so a nigga was good. I didn't know how that muthafucka had snuck his piece in, but he'd done it. That nigga was also by himself which was a brave ass move. I guess he wanted to murder me to reclaim his pride. My guess was he had followed us to the strip club and then decided to sneak some shots off while he thought I was busy watching some ass. What he didn't know was a nigga like me was always observing the scene. Ass never distracted me. It wasn't *ever* going to be that easy to put some steel in me. Hell nah. Now I had to figure out how I was going to deal with that nigga Duke.

*   *   *

"Damn that nigga acted like he was gon' just get away wit' that shit if you didn't have yo' peice on you. Shit, I was strapped too and I know that Deniro and Mel was. Like we won't gon' tear that mufuckin' club up if he shot you!" Cane was fired up. "Niggas be on some suicidal ass shit these days."

We'd stopped at the "boardroom" on Candler Road to regroup and shit. That was our spot on the first floor of an apartment complex that OG Uncle Pete had taken over back in the days when he and my grandfather first started the Cues. It was the Cues headquarters, so that's where we handled and discussed Cue business. My niggas had rolled a few much needed blunts and we had the cipher going. I was sipping straight from a bottle of Patron Silver because shit had just gone from zero to one hundred in no time. The life that I lived often resulted in those crazy life and death situations, but each time they fucked with me in a different way. That time I thought about Baby and the fact that she'd just turned her back on me and shit. I had to erase all of her doubts and fears somehow. Life was short as hell and I was determined to fight for her. What had just happened made it clear to me that I needed her bad as hell. She'd said one thing with her mouth, but I knew that she really felt something totally different with her heart.

"What you gon' tell Duke nigga?" Deniro asked as he flicked ashes from the blunt into the ash tray.

"I'm sure somebody saw that shit and he gon' be askin' questions," Mel spoke up with a freshly rolled blunt between his fingers. He lit it, took a few pulls and passed it to me.

I hit the aromatic, loud ass weed and it tasted fruity like Skittles. After I inhaled deeply, I blew circles of thick smoke out of my mouth before answering my dude.

"Man, Duke don't put no fear in me, but I'on really know exactly what I'm gon' do yet. That was his fam, so he gon' feel some type of way. Still, I'm who I am and he gotta know what's gon' happen if he bring it to me. For sho'. Shit. I'on give a fuck how long he been a Cue. I'm Diablo's son and if he bring it to me, he gon' have to deal wit' me and my pops."

"And us nigga!" Cane yelled holding a Sprite bottle in his hand.

We all knew that it was full of Lean.

"Hell yeah my nigga. We got yo' back. It's whatever," Mel said as he leaned back in his seat.

"Damn, I'm fucked up," Deniro said with a sigh. "It's time to make sure them niggas did the last drop and shit." He stood up and stretched.

"Hell yeah, ya'll niggas handle that and do the count. Oh yeah, and make sure ya'll check up on that clientele in North Carolina and shit. They just copped ten last time, but this time they want twenty," I said as I got up and passed the blunt to Cane. "I'm out."

I pounded my niggas up as they agreed to handle shit for the night and with those niggas in Charlotte. The warm night air hit my face as I checked my cell to see what time it was. It was after three am, so I decided against calling Mackie. I'd hit her up later and hopefully she'd talk to me. I'd just emptied my clip in some lame ass nigga and his cousin was my Cue brother, but all that was on my mind was Baby. Damn, I loved that girl and I wasn't going to stop trying until she was down for a nigga like I needed her to be.

Chapter 5

Mackie

I slept late as hell the next day because I'd tossed and turned all night. Not only was I heartbroken over Zy, but it just felt like something wasn't right. I couldn't quite put my finger on what it was. When I woke up I found the note from Princess saying that she took Tre to the hospital for his physical therapy. She'd recently put the twins in daycare, so they would be gone until at least six o' clock. It was quiet and peaceful and I was glad. My appetite was nonexistent, so I decided to just chill in front of the TV and wallow in my misery. Truth be told, I missed Zy. The sound of my cell phone ringing got my attention and when I saw my best friend Beyanka's phone number, I almost didn't answer. Then I thought about how much I missed her too.

"Hello," I said knowing that she'd sense that something was wrong with me immediately.

"Heyyyy bitch! Why the fuck you soundin' all sad and shit?" She asked in her flamboyant way of talking.

My bestie was nothing like me. That heifer was wild as hell and she didn't give a damn who knew it.

Everything she did was over the top and that was kind of what I liked the most about her. She wasn't afraid to say or do whatever. She had no filter and she had absolutely no chill.

"Me and Zy broke up," I said filling her in on our weekend at the Lake and our recent argument.

"Wow, have you talked to him?" She asked.

"Nah. He called me earlier, but I was sleep."

"You gon' call him back?"

"I don't know."

"Well, I got a surprise for you," she said in a sly voice.

"A surprise? What?"

The doorbell rang and I got up to peek out of the window. I saw a white car that looked like a taxi. Who the hell could that be? At first I thought it was Zy, but I doubted that he'd be riding in a taxi.

"Girl, I asked you a question," I said looking through the peephole.

When I saw my best friend standing there, I pulled the door open and we both started screaming. I grabbed her and hugged her so tight that she probably couldn't even breathe.

"Oh my God! You're actually here! How the hell did you keep that shit from me bitch?" I asked finally smiling for the first time since everything had gone down with Zy.

She laughed slyly. "I planned it with your mom. Tre and his wife said it was cool for me to come down for a couple weeks. I decided to just catch a taxi from the airport since I had the address."

"Well, come on in girl. Let's catch up," I said closing the door behind her after we went inside with her bags.

Beyanka was gorgeous with her smooth, dark brown skin, exotic, slanted cognac colored eyes, and full, pouty lips. She was about 5'8 and to me she looked like a super model. The only thing was that she had ass for days. Her upper body wasn't big at all, but her hips and ass made up for that and it was all real. She also loved her weaves. My boo would spend a grip for some Malaysian Remy and the longer the better. Not only that, but she kept her fake lash extensions long and her face was always beat to perfection. She loved clothes and shoes and that was why she had like six bags with her.

After laughing and talking about what was going on in Richmond, the doorbell rang again. I wondered who the hell that could've been. It was only three o' clock in the afternoon, so I wasn't expecting Tre and Princess to be back so soon. Besides, they wouldn't be ringing the doorbell of their own crib anyway. Then it occurred to me that it was probably Zy. I looked through the peephole and realized that I was right.

"Who is it?" Beyanka asked.

I sighed. "It's Zy."

"Open the door bitch!"

I swung the door open and tried not to show how I was really feeling. He needed to think that I would be okay without him even if I didn't. When he stepped inside I introduced him to Beyanka.

"Hello Zy," she said with a smile as she shook his hand.

"Hi Beyanka. It's nice to meet you. I'm glad to finally meet one of Baby's friends," he said with a smile on his face too.

"Baby?" Beyanka's smile turned into a sly one. "Hmm. So, she's Baby huh?" She looked at me. "Somebody's feelin' you mama."

"I'm feelin' the shit outta your girl. She ain't tryna fuck wit' me like that though. Is she always hot and cold like that bestie? Help me figure her out." He glanced at me and then focused back on Beyanka.

I had a salty ass look on my face. "You know it's not like that Zy. You..."

Beyanka cut me off. "Yup, she's always been like that. I can see right through her front though. She's in love wit' you and she really wants to be wit' you. She just gotta learn to let go."

He sighed. "Yes. I been tellin' her that she needs to just relax and let shit flow, but she won't do it. Yesterday she completely cut me off and shit because...we'll, I'm sure she told you about my ex."

"And what happened at the party," I cut him off.

"Yeah, she did, but I don't understand..."

I cut my eyes at my friend. "You don't understand because you love thugs. I know you're not gonna take his side. You don't even know him."

Beyanka rolled her eyes at me. "You need to stop tryna play so damn hard. You were just tellin' me how much you love this man. Don't let some bitch break you two apart. I'm here now, so that hoe can try to act like she 'bout that life if she want to."

"Listen to your girl yo'," Zy said reaching for my hand.

I pulled away.

He sighed. "Can you go wit' me outside please."

"Uh, you two can stay right here. I'll go upstairs and give you some privacy," Beyanka spoke up as she grabbed her bags. "Where should I put my stuff Mackie?"

"Oh, no, it's cool. You're good. We'll just go outside for a minute then you'll have your girl back. I know ya'll probably got plans or something," Zy said heading toward the door like he just knew I'd go with him.

"I didn't agree to go…" I started with my arms across my chest, but Beyanka interrupted my stubbornness.

"Girl, go wit' the man outside. Gosh! What the hell is wrong wit' you?"

I flipped her the bird as I walked backwards. Then I turned to follow him outside.

"What did you want me to come out here for?" I asked with an attitude. "I told you that it's…"

"I almost got killed last night. Me and the niggas were at Magic City and shit when that nigga Ro, Duke's cousin who tried to holla at you at the party, walked up on me with a gun and shit. I shot his ass before he could shoot me and I got the word today that he's dead and shit. Now, at this point I should be concerned about what kinda war I done started within my crew, but that shit don't matter. All my mind keeps going back to is the fact that I could've died without makin' shit right wit' you. I know that my lifestyle is dangerous ma. I get that, but it still don't stop me from lovin' you. It shouldn't stop you either. If anything it should make you hold on to me tighter. That shit should just make our bond stronger. I ain't gon' give up on you without a fight ma. Shit, look at my pops and Yanna. Look at Princess and Tre and Daren and Reco. They beat the mufuckin' odds Baby and we can too. I need you and you know that. Don't give up on a nigga. I got you ma and I ain't gon' do nothin' but love you until the day I die. That's all I wanna be able to do. Just let me…please. Just let me love you Baby."

There were tears streaming down my cheeks and I felt so bad for what I'd said to him the day before. If I had lost him I would've been so devastated and there was no way I would've been able to forgive myself.

"I'm so sorry Zy," I cried and pulled him into my arms. The familiar scent of his cologne of choice invaded my nostrils and comforted me. "I love you and I'm gonna try babe, okay. I promise that I'm gonna try."

"Good. That's all I wanna hear Baby. That's all the fuck a nigga want. Damn, I love you," he said as he slid his hand in the back pocket of my jeans.

At first I thought he was just copping a feel on my ass, but when he removed his hand from my pocket there was something he'd left behind. When we broke our embrace I reached in my pocket and pulled out a key.

"What's this?" I asked eyeing it curiously.

There was a huge, cocky grin on his face and his eyes danced with mischief as he shrugged his shoulders. "I'on know. It was already in your pocket."

"No it wasn't."

When he turned and looked to his left, my eyes followed his to a cute little two door, baby blue Mini Cooper. I glanced down at the key and put two and two together. The key did have Mini written on it in gold with the little wings.

"It's yours," he said as he stared into my shocked face.

"It's mine?" I asked as I walked down the steps to take a good look at the car he was giving me.

He followed me and then the smile on his face faded when I said what I said next.

"I can't take that Zy. It's too much." I tried giving him the key back, but he didn't take it.

"Nope. Give it to your friend Beyanka then," he said with his hands in the pockets of his jeans.

"What?" I asked not knowing why he would give me a car so soon in our relationship. "Are you trying to buy me Zy? I agreed to take you back. You didn't have to get me a car."

He shook his head. "No. I ain't tryna buy you ma. You'll need a car when you go to school and work and shit, so why not? It's not flashy, but it's still a nice, luxury ride. I thought you'd like it."

"I love it. It's just. It's just too much."

"No, it's not too much Baby. Nothin' is or will ever be too much when it comes to you. I'm sorry if buyin' you a car offends you, but get prepared to be offended a lot. I wanna spoil you and that's something that you're gonna have to get used to. Don't take it as me tryna buy or control you. I love you because you're you. I don't wanna ever change who you are, or make your feel like you gotta bow down to me. The niggas in the streets bow down to me, but I bow down to you. I got enough control baby, so I wanna be able to lose control wit' you. I just want you to be able to do that shit wit' me. I'm your nigga. You deserve everything that I give you and you don't owe me shit. Just love me and let me love you. How many times I gotta say the same shit to you before you understand that I'm for real?" He leaned over and kissed me before I could say anything else.

"Thank you Zy, but how am I gonna explain this car to my mom? I mean Tre and P. won't be surprised, but I'm sure that she'll advise me to give it back."

"You're welcome Baby. Just tell her that I won't take it back. Plus, I didn't get you this car because you broke up wit' me yesterday or because of what happened last night. I got it because you need it to get around and I want you to be safe. It's crazy out here ma and I don't want you on the bus, or the train at night. If I could be wit' you every second it would be different, but I know that I can't. I'm over protective and I can't help it. I'm just like that. It just so happened that Ju finished the custom paint job today and shit. I was gonna give it to you whether you agreed to take me back or not."

"Okay," I nodded and walked toward the house.

"Where you goin' shorty?" Zy asked behind me.

"To get Bey so we can go for a ride in my new whip. You need me to drop you off somewhere?" I looked back with a wink.

He laughed. "Yeah. Take me to my nigga Cane's crib."

*   *   *

"Bitch, this car is too damn cute. Your ass is crazy. Ain't no way in the world I would've offered to give the key back." Beyanka just had to say something when Zy told her about me trying to give the car back.

"I told her to give it to you then," Zy laughed and then put his hand on my thigh.

I glanced over at him with a grin. "Get your hand off me."

"Nope," he said defiantly as he squeezed.

"Hmm, give me this mufucka if you want to. You won't get it back," Beyanka spat.

"Make a left," Zy said giving me directions when I could've easily used the GPS on my phone.

"I'm gonna need the GPS to get back anyway," I said once we pulled up in front of Cane's crib.

He lived in a nice, big, two story brick house in a gated community in Decatur and when Bey saw it she was ready to pounce. One thing about her was she loved a thug, but not just any thug. She loved those thugs who had deep pockets, so she only fucked with ballers and shot callers. Cane was right up her alley from the looks of his crib as well as the Mercedes and Audi truck parked in the driveway.

"Damn, introduce me to your boy," she said ready to get out of the car so that she could prance around that nigga.

I shook my head. "I knew that was coming."

"Cuz you know your girl," Bey laughed.

By the time we got out of the car Cane was already outside. When he saw Beyanka his eyes almost popped out of their sockets. He was staring at her ass hard and I knew that she was attracted to him too. He was a red bone with gray eyes so he was just her type. Her type was the total opposite of mine, which made our friendship work. I never had to worry about her trying to fuck with my man. Not only would she not be physically attracted to a man that I was with, but she was also loyal, so she wouldn't have done it anyway.

"Damn!" Cane said as he came closer. "Who the fuck is this sexy ass mufucka here Zy?" He was smiling and his iced out grill was gleaming in the sunlight.

Beyanka's eyes were on him and she was looking at that nigga like she was blinded by the glare of his bling. Not only were his teeth iced out, but he had on an iced out chain, watch and pinky ring. His True Religion outfit and Jordan's had her calculating everything in her head. I could tell by how she was staring at him.

"Mmm, I can speak for myself. I'm Beyanka and what's yo' name, wit' yo' fine ass."

"I'm Cane baby girl. It's nice to meet you."

They shook hands and were both grinning in one another's face.

Zy cleared his throat, but Cane still didn't acknowledge him. I'd met Cane before and I was aware of his reputation with the ladies. I figured that Bey could handle herself. She was used to dealing with dudes like him and she would only be there for two weeks anyway. She wasn't the type to fall for the okey doke, so I wasn't worried. If anything she was going to fuck with him and get some of his coins before returning to Richmond. It was going to be all fun, so I figured she didn't really need a warning.

"Uh, what you 'bout to get into sexy?" Cane asked Bey like me and Zy were not even there.

"I'on know. What we 'bout to get into Mackie?" She asked without taking her eyes off Cane.

"Well…" I glanced at Zy.

"If ya'll wanna chill and smoke or something it's up to ya'll," Zy said sensing that I wanted his approval before we imposed.

"Okay, you wanna chill Bey?" I asked knowing damn well she wanted to.

"Hell yeah," she agreed.

*   *   *

Zyon

Baby and her girl were geeking hard off that Gas that nigga Cane had rolled up. I could sense that nigga's attraction to old girl and it was nothing new. I wasn't a blind nigga. She was my girl's best friend and shit, but I could see all that ass she was toting. I knew that was my dude's type all day, so he was on it.

"Damn, that ass is so fuckin' fat," Cane said under his breath to me when we broke off to the kitchen for a quick exchange.

I had got up to get a beer and he had to come into the kitchen to give me his opinion of Beyanka.

"Yeah, but you know how that go man. I ain't 'bout to be gawkin' over my girl's best friend's ass," I laughed as I twisted the top off of my Bud Light.

"I know my nigga, but I can't keep my eyes off that shit. Not only is that ass fat as hell, but she's actually pretty and shit. Damn," he shook his head. "Your girl Mackie gotta put a nigga on."

"Put yourself on man. Shorty's right there in your face showin' you that she's interested nigga." I took a swig of my beer and realized that I'd almost polished that shit off in one swallow.

"Yeah, you know how that shit go man. I'on want her tellin' her girl how I am yo'. She might not fuck wit' me."

I shrugged my shoulders. "Beyanka seem like she's the kinda chick who make up her own mind 'bout what she wanna do and shit, especially who she wanna fuck."

Cane nodded. "You right man. I'on know why shawty got me all fucked up and shit. That ain't like me."

"Nah nigga. That ain't like you at all." I couldn't help but chuckle. Old girl had my boy all nervous and shit. That nigga actually cared about her knowing that he was a hoe.

"You actin' like this and you ain't even touched her yet. Hmm. If you get some of that you might be whipped."

He smirked at me. "Nigga please. I ain't capable of bein' whipped. I ain't like you. All sensitive when it comes to chicks and shit. Fuck that."

"I'm glad that I'm whipped. That's some hard ass shit to do to a nigga like me, so Baby gotta be special."

"I feel you homey. We both young and shit. You sure you wanna settle down? You what...eighteen? I'm twenty. We got our whole life for that shit?"

"Or do we man? Not with the lifestyle we live. That shit don't matter man. Age don't mean a damn thing when you love somebody."

"Well I guess I'll worry 'bout love when I feel it. Until then I'm enjoyin' just fuckin' these hoes."

I shook my head at Cane. "That's my girl's best friend and shit man. Don't put me in a fucked up position wit' her. Be straight up wit' shorty."

"Damn nigga. You breakin' the bro code and shit."

"When it comes to Baby, fuck the damn bro code. It ain't no bro code."

"Oh damn nigga. You far gone and shit."

We laughed.

"Let's go chill wit' them for a minute and then we gotta discuss what's gonna go down wit' Duke. I gotta hit my pops up and see what he thinks. You know Duke is close as hell to Reco and shit. I gotta do shit the right way. You feel me?" I asked knowing that shit could really go left if I decided to tell Duke about that nigga Ro.

"Word. I feel you. A'ight man, c'mon."

I grabbed another beer before joining them in the living room. There was a smile on my face, but I didn't know what the hell was going to go down. I was used to fighting wars against other crews, not against my niggas I'd been running with since I was fifteen. Damn, but what would Duke have wanted me to do. Let his folk kill me and shit? That was not going to happen. As far as I was concerned I didn't feel the need to explain shit. If he found out he just found out, but I needed to control how and when he did. I didn't need another sneak attack attempt on my life. I liked to know when that shit was coming so I could avoid death a little bit longer. When I glanced over at my girl, I knew that going about shit the wrong way would be a very bad idea. If she lost me it would kill her and I knew it. That was why she was so cautious about letting me have her heart.

"I love you," she whispered in my ear after I sat down next to her.

"I love you too bae," I confirmed before giving her a kiss.

"Aww, ya'll are so adorable," Beyanka said staring at us like she longed for what we had.

"What? That lovey dovey shit is so lame," Cane said playfully. "This nigga stay cakin'."

"If you found the right chick you'd be all lame and lovey dovey too," Beyanka challenged him.

"Oh, so you think a nigga like me is capable of bein' a lame?" Cane had a doubtful look on his face.

"If that's what you call it," she said. "I mean, if I put it on your ass *and* hold you down, you'll be buyin' me cars and shit too."

Cane laughed like that shit was so hilarious. "What? Shawty's confident and shit. A'ight. How about we go on in the room now and try out the put it on me part. You can hold me down later."

We all laughed at that, but I knew that the fun wasn't going to last. Shit was about to get serious as hell. All I knew was that I planned to still be standing when the smoke cleared.

Chapter 6

Mackie

I didn't want to leave Zy because of what he'd told me about the night before, but I knew that he had to do what he had to do. He had certain duties in the streets that I had to accept whether I liked it or not. As scared as I was of losing him, he was right, I loved him anyway. Knowing that he could've lost his life just reassured me of that love and the fact that I needed to spend as much time as I could with him. Just in case his lifestyle did take him away from me; not being with him in the meantime was only going to make me miserable.

"I'm gon' fuck that nigga Cane," Beyanka said breaking through my thoughts.

"I knew you wanted to fuck him. I could tell by the way you kept staring at him."

She laughed. "I would've gone ahead and did it, but I was like nah. I'll wait a couple days. Make him sweat me and spend a lil' money. I'm just tryna go somewhere tonight. I know that it's Tuesday, but this is ATL shawty. I know it's always some shit to get into. Good thing your boo came through wit' the whip. That shit was right on time."

"True. You know my mama is gonna trip about this car," I said thinking about the fact that my mom would be back on Friday.

"Does she know about Zy?" Beyanka asked knowing damn well I hadn't told my mom about him.

"Girl, you know how Sylvia is. She is not gonna be happy about me bein' with a dude like Zy and she's really gonna chew me out about accepting this car. I'm gonna tell her about him. I mean I have to explain where this car came from. I'm just not looking forward to that shit."

"I'll be here, so you'll have me there to help you out. Zy seems to really care about you regardless of his lifestyle. I can tell that he's serious about you. When your mom sees you two together she'll understand it. If not, then oh well. You have to live your own life. You're a grown woman now."

"You're right Bey, but my mother will never look at it that way. I'm her only child and she don't play about me doing what she calls dumb shit."

Beyanka had three brothers and two sisters, so she came from a big family. Her mother Regina was a no nonsense hair stylist who had raised her children to be close. She made a good living, but she seemed to not be able to let go of her street side. Therefore all of her children could be pretty brash and outspoken. Bey was the next to the youngest, so she was well protected by her older siblings. I kind of envied that she had what I'd always longed for. Still, she was like my sister, so I'd adopted her family too.

"What is the problem with Zy? You seem to be holdin' back wit' him."

"I really care too deeply for him in such a short amount of time. Then the type of lifestyle he lives makes things complicated. I'm just scared that he's gonna be ripped out of my life when I least expect it and it's gonna rock my world. It makes me think about what happened to my mother. She was pregnant with me when my daddy's body was found with a bullet in his head. I don't know if I'm as strong as her. She warned me all my life to stay away from guys like Zy and here I am in love with the type of man she told me to avoid. That's just my damn luck." I sighed as I thought about how out of control I was when it came to my feelings for Zy. Usually I was able to not feel when I didn't want to. When it came to him all I could do was feel.

"I know that you're a control freak, so when you can't control something you feel like you have to separate yourself from it. Obviously you can't control this and it ain't shit wrong wit' that. You can't control everything. You're a good person Mackie and you deserve real love. I think Zy really loves you. Hmm. You know how I feel about men and love. If I can see it, you know that's some genuine shit." She smiled at me. "Don't let his ex girl or your mama mess up what's meant for you."

She was right. I was going to just tell my mother all about Zy and put my foot down with her. Who I loved and wanted to be with was my business. As far as Kia was concerned, I was not going to let her win. Her goal was to break us up and although he didn't want her, she just didn't want us to be together. I wasn't going to give that bitch the satisfaction. The more she tried to break us up, the tighter I was going to cling to him. That hoe was going to see that I wasn't going anywhere and that would eventually motivate her to move on with her pathetic ass life. For the time being I was going to kick back and have some fun with my best friend.

*   *   *

"And when did you start smokin' weed bitch?" Bey asked as she did my make up for our night out.

"What took you so long to ask?" I laughed.

She laughed too. "I just thought about it. Good thing Zy gave you that fat loud pack. I was gonna ask where I could cop from. That's crazy. We've been friends forever and I could never get you to smoke wit' me. You fall in love wit' a nigga and he can talk your ass into anything."

"For your info, he didn't talk me into it. I asked him to hit the blunt."

"Well excuse me Miss bad ass Mackie. There you go girl. Look in the mirror," she said with a smile of approval on her face. "I did that bitch."

"Yes you did," I said when I caught a glimpse of my reflection. "Thank you for not over doing it. You know how I am."

"Yeah, I know. I do your makeup the way I wouldn't do mine."

We both laughed at that.

"Well, let me finish beatin' my face to perfection and then we can go," Bey said behind me as I left the bathroom.

"K. I'll be downstairs."

On my way down I ran into Princess coming up the stairs. "Wow. Look at you. Where are ya'll going on a Tuesday night?"

"Thanks. Central Station or something like that. It's in East Point."

"Oh, that's a hood ass spot."

"That's Bey's type of party then," I said with a sly grin.

"Mmm hmm. Well, ya'll be careful out there. I know you ain't used to driving around here, so make sure you stay alert. Atlanta got some of the worst damn drivers. I love the car, but you have to tell your mom the truth about it," she said for the umpteenth time since she saw it in the drive way.

I nodded. "Okay P. I told you that I would and I am when she gets here. For now let me enjoy it."

Princess smiled. "A'ight. Well, have fun. I know I am." She winked at me. "The twins are sleep and when ya'll leave it's 'bout to be on up in here."

"Ewww." I frowned up my face at her playful reference to sexing up my cousin.

She was laughing hard as hell as she walked away.

When I got downstairs I called Zy. It was hard not to worry about him. Being with a man like him was going to take some getting used to on my part. Every second I wondered if he was still alive.

"Baby, what's up ma?" I could hear the smile in his voice and that made me smile from ear to ear.

He really made me happy and there was no way I could deny that.

"Nothin' much. Just waitin' for Bey to finish getting' ready," I said as I sat down on the sofa.

I had kept it simple with a pair of light blue True Religion skinny jeans with rips down the legs, a cute, low cut peach colored top and light brown Jimmy Choo sandals with a two inch heel, just in case shit got crunk in the club.

"Okay. Where're ya'll goin'?"

"Central Station."

"Ohhhh, okay. Uh, if you didn't like Duke's party you won't like it out there either. Believe me." He chuckled and I wondered if he just didn't want me to go out.

"Well, that's the spot Bey wants to go to, so I won't be a party pooper. Besides, it's Tuesday, maybe it won't be too much goin' on."

"Hmm, this is the A. It's gon' be a wild ass party any day of the week. For sho. Just be careful out there ma. I might pop up, so make sure you on yo' shit. You know what happened the last time I caught a nigga talkin' to you." He said it teasingly, but I knew just how serious that shit had got and I didn't want it to happen again.

"You ain't gotta worry bae. I know how to act."

"I know. Well, I gotta handle some shit, but I'll hit you wit' a text if I decide to roll out there. A'ight?"

"Okay," I said not wanting to end our conversation. Something told me that he was going to handle the situation with Duke and I was stressing about it. Damn, I knew that he was hard to a certain extent, but even the hardest nigga could be penetrated by a bullet.

"I love you Baby and don't you be worryin' 'bout me. I'm gon' be good. A'ight."

"Alright. I love you too Zy."

He hung up and I wanted to call him right back. Bey finally came down the stairs dressed in practically nothing.

"Let's go boo!" She said it like she was so excited.

I shook my head. "Where'd you hear about the spot we're goin' to?"

"My brother Rock went when he came down here last summer. He said some niggas were shootin' in the parking lot, but he had a ball."

I gave her a sideways glance as we walked outside. "Really Bey? You can't be serious. You wanna go to a spot where your brother said somebody was shooting when he went?"

She shrugged her shoulders indifferently. "Niggas always be shootin' at the hot spots. That's the norm."

As I opened the car door I couldn't help but shake my head. My friend was too damn much and I kind of hoped that Zy *would* show up at the club.

*   *   *

It was almost two am and so far we were having a ball and nothing had happened…yet. Of course I was just a little annoyed because of Bey's friendliness with dudes. They thought because she wanted a drink or to dance up on them, that I did. It was really frustrating me that I had to keep telling the friends of the dudes she was freaking on that I didn't want to dance with them. I mean, I didn't mind dancing, but I'd never been into dancing up on strange men.

Suddenly some chick kept bumping me as she threw her ass on some dude. The dance floor was packed so I tried to move out of her way, but she kept moving too. I rolled my eyes and decided to just leave the dance floor since I wasn't really into it anyway. All of the sweaty partiers were bumping and swaying to the beat while I just stood there. Why was I getting mad at them? That was what the dance floor was for. At least Bey was having a good time. Before I could make it to a chair to sit down, I felt someone grab my arm from behind.

I figured that it was Bey, so I turned around to see what she wanted. When I turned I felt a crushing blow to my face. My instinct was to fight back although I couldn't even see who I was fighting with. My fists were going a hundred miles per hour and I knew that I was making contact with something. When I was finally able to open my eyes everything was blurry, but I saw Bey grab whoever had hit me in the face. She was fucking that bitch up while I tried my best to focus.

"C'mon Bey!" I yelled trying to get her away from the chick. At the same time I was kicking that hoe. As I did some other bitch jumped in and I ended up fighting her.

Next thing I knew I felt someone grab me and I was kicking and screaming to get away.

"Let me go!" I yelled when it dawned on me that it was that bitch Kia and her friend Melanie. "Let me fuckin' go!"

"That bitch hit my girl in the face first! Shit! I'm gon' beat yo' ass again. I'll find you bitch!" Bey screamed as she moved her body around wildly in an attempt to get away from security.

"Fuck both of ya'll hoes! I told that prissy bitch I was gon' fuck her up if I saw her again! Yeah, you ain't wit' yo' nigga now! He's probably out fuckin' some other bitch! That's what he do best! You fallin' for that game he be spittin' huh? He cheated on me and he'll cheat on yo' boogie ass too!" Kia spat as another bouncer held her back.

"Is that you why you want him back bitch?! Huh! Fuck you!" I yelled as the bouncers pulled me and Bey away and headed toward the door.

They took us outside first.

"Go to your cars now!" The tall, dark complexioned bouncer with the huge barrel chest yelled as he pointed toward the parking lot.

"Fuck this shit!" Bey spat as she grabbed my hand. "You okay? You need me to drive? Damn, look at your eye! So, that was Zy's ex huh?"

"Hell yeah," I said as I reached in my pocket for the key.

She took it from me and then glanced back to see that the bouncer was waiting for us to leave before they sent Kia and Melanie out.

"Don't even worry 'bout what that bitch said. She's just hatin' on you and Zy. That bitch's gon' get hers before I leave. That's on everything I fuckin' love!"

"I can't believe that hoe. She was the one who was bumpin' me the whole fuckin' time. If I had seen her face I would've known what it was, but she meant to sneak up on me. Scared ass bitch." I was tired of people thinking that they could just run all over me.

It was about time that I showed muthafuckas that I was not a soft, punk ass bitch. It was no way I was going to continue to be pushed around. I wasn't a little girl anymore and I wasn't going to let some hoe just attack me over my man and get away with it. Hell nah.

There would no repeat of my abusive history. I would no longer be the victim. I was going to flip that shit and turn the tables. The next bitch who fucked with me was going to get more than my fucking fists and I meant that shit.

*   *   *

I was up by 10 o' clock the next morning anxious to tell Zy about what had happened with Kia. His phone had been going to the voicemail since I left the club, so I decided to go to his pent house. I was worried that something had happened to him and I was thinking about what Kia had said about him cheating on me. Before I left I told Bey where I was going. She was still wrapped up under the covers so I knew that she didn't care about what I was about to do. I was still mad as hell at that bitch Kia. When I looked at my eye in the mirror, I wanted to beat that bitch's ass all over again. I tried my best to cover the bruise up with some makeup, but it was still slightly swollen even after icing it for hours.

It was a good thing I was able to open it so that I could see well enough to drive. I just hoped it would be back to normal before my mother got there. Tre and Princess hadn't even seen it, so I was going to try to avoid them as much as possible. Shit, I had two days to doctor it up as best I could, or come up with some story to explain it away. I damn sure didn't want anyone thinking that Zy was beating on me, nor did I want them to know that I had fought some chick because of him.

I rung the doorbell and waited anxiously for him to come to the door. As I stood there my heart raced because I just knew that there was some bitch in there with him. Last time I talked to him he had told me that he was going to come to the club. He hadn't even bothered to text or call to check on me. I did see his Charger and Mercedes SUV in their parking spots, so I knew that he was there. When he finally opened the door in a pair of gray sweats and no shirt, I literally leaped into his arms.

"Baby, what, what the hell happened to your eye?" He asked as he carried me inside.

I looked at him as he sat down on the sofa and placed me comfortably in his lap. "I'm just glad that you're okay, but why didn't you call or text me."

"I dropped my phone in the fuckin' toilet and shit last night. I was drunk as fuck and that shit was in my back pocket. I had forgot and shit. I woke up a lil' while ago and realized that I need to go to Verizon and get another damn phone. I had my other phone in there, but I use that one for you know...Anyway, I was gonna stop by and let you know what was up. Shit, your number was saved in that phone…so…Now, what happened to your eye ma?" He gave me a stern look.

"What happened with Duke?" I asked wanting to know that first, because it seemed more pressing than my little fight with his ex and her friend.

"I wanna know what the fuck happened to your eye and then we'll talk about that."

"I ran into your girl Kia at Central Station last night. She snuck up behind me and grabbed me. When I turned around she stole me in the face. We got into it and then Bey jumped on that bitch. I didn't want us to get in trouble, so I tried to grab Bey and get out of there, but then Kia's girl Melanie jumped on me. To make a long story short security made us leave before they made them leave. She's been all on Facebook talking about how she beat my ass and shit. She also said that you were probably out cheatin' on me…"

"Don't let her put that shit in your head and fuck that Facebook gangsta shit she talkin'. Don't feed into Kia's bullshit ma. I wasn't out cheatin' on you. I just wanted to give you your time wit' your friend. It ain't like she gon' be here that long. I didn't want you to think I was tryna keep tabs on you, 'cause I trust you. Shit, now I wish I had went. The shit wit' Duke is on pause for now. Ro's folks live in Alabama and they sent his body there today. Duke went down there and he gon' be there until the funeral. My pops said it's best I just let that nigga know what happened. We gon' strap up and just do what we gotta do if he trip about that shit. He also said he gon' holla at Reco, since he and Duke are real close. He was tellin' me 'bout what happened to Tre and I don't want that type of shit to pop off again."

I nodded in understanding. I knew that my cousin Tre had got shot in the chest a few months back and was in critical condition because he had killed Zy's father best friend Ace some years back. It was all over Tre's wife Princess. Princess had been fucking with Ace when Tre was locked up and Ace couldn't let go. He had tried to kill them both one night, but Tre ended up killing him instead. Tre had kept it from Diablo and Ace's sister. When Ace's sister found out recently after reading a book that Tre had written called The Forbidden Fruit that chronicled the true story of himself, Diablo and their crew, she shot him without warning. I knew all of the facts because of course my mother had told me the whole story.

"Yeah, we wouldn't want that to happen bae. I know that Diablo will have your back and I hope they'll understand that you were just defending yourself," I said planting a kiss on his lips. "I missed you so much and I was so worried."

"I missed you more and don't worry about me Baby, I'm a G. Now, back to your eye. I can't believe that bitch did that shit! When I get my hands on her…"

"No, I don't want you to get in any shit fuckin' wit' that dumb ass broad," I said quickly. "Something's gonna have to give though, 'cause I can't be worried about looking over my damn shoulder all the time."

He was furious and I could tell, but for some reason I didn't want him to put his hands on her. I wanted to get that bitch back and that time it wasn't going to be some scuffle. There had to be something else I could do to get at her, but at the moment I couldn't think of anything other than shooting her ass. Then again, I wasn't some cold blooded killer like Zy, so although I'd contemplated asking him for a gun, that was out of the question. I'd just have to deal with that bitch without killing her.

"And I don't want you to have to do that either." He sighed. "Where your girl Beyanka at?"

"She's still in the bed. She sleeps late."

"What ya'll got planned for the day?"

"Nothing really. I don't wanna go nowhere with my eye like this, but I don't wanna stay in the house so Tre and Princess can see it either."

"Okay, you go to the crib and drop your car off. You and your girl pack a bag for the night while I go get a phone. I'll scoop you and ya'll can chill wit' me and Cane. He'd love to have ol' girl to himself for a lil' while. I'll hide you out 'till your eye looks better." He kissed my bruised eye gently. "I still wanna put my hands on that bitch for touchin' you though. I feel like that shit was my fault."

"Nah babe. It ain't your fault that bitch won't let go. Hmm, I know for a fact that shit wit' you is just that good. I can't let go either."

"I ain't gon' let you let me go. Now, how 'bout a quickie and shit. Black eye or not...yo' ass is sexy."

Chapter 7

Beyanka

Damn, that nigga Zy was living good as hell. His hot ass pent house was laid. If I was doing the shit I did in Richmond and he wasn't my girl's boo, I'd sick the jack boys on his ass. I was thinking of doing that shit to Cane. It would be easy as hell to get my brothers and their crew of goons to come out to the A and wipe them niggas out, but I liked Cane. That nigga was cool as a fan, so I wasn't on that scheming shit. However, I was trying to spend some of that nigga's bread.

After he and Zy told me and Mackie to chill while they cooked, it was time for a shopping spree. I was full as hell because those niggas had turned the crib into Red Lobster. They had hooked up some crab legs, lobster tails, shrimp scampi, potatoes, corn and even those little cheddar biscuits. That shit was bomb.

"So, you *can* cook," Mackie had said with a happy little smile on her face as she stared lovingly at Zy.

"Told you," Zy said smiling right back at her. "But you always doubtin' a nigga."

It was good to see my best friend happy with somebody. Since I'd known her she tried so hard to be straight laced and into the books, so she didn't really have a life. She'd gone out with Chris for a little while, but there was no real passion there. I saw all of the passion in the world between her and Zy though. Deep down beneath the surface, I wanted that for me, but I didn't think I deserved it. I wasn't cut from the same cloth as Mackie. She'd been through some things that she never had talked to me about it and I knew that they bothered her. Zy seemed to make her forget all about those things. I'd been Mackie's friends since we were in the third grade and I could never make her forget. He was definitely good for her.

"I want to eat yo' pussy so fuckin' bad shawty," Cane whispered in my ear for the tenth time since I'd been there.

"A'ight. You can do way more than that if you take me to Phipps and spend some coins," I said putting that nigga on blast in front of Mackie and Zy.

"Hmm, no beatin' around the bush huh?" Zy laughed as he gutted a Swisher.

"Hell nah," I smiled slyly. "This nigga ain't beatin' around the bush about wantin' some of this pussy, so why should I act like I don't want him to spend some money. This good ass pussy ain't free and this nigga ain't gon' sit here and pretend like he ain't never paid for no pussy before." I stood up in front of Cane and put the pussy all up in his face. "I promise you that this is gon' be the first time your money will be well fuckin' spent nigga. You may think you had some good pussy before, but I bet you'll start to question all of that shit after you get some of this. I love to fuck, but my pussy don't get wet without an incentive. I'm a sexy bitch, but I'm a smart bitch. So, what's up?"

Cane stood up, grabbed her arm and playfully pulled her toward the door. "C'mon shawty let's go. Y'en said nothin' but a word. After that I want you to back up all that shit you talkin'."

Zy and Mackie were just shaking their heads at us as they laughed.

"The two of you are perfect together," Mackie said with her eyes on me.

"Yeah, ya'll niggas need to be on a fuckin' reality show," Zy chuckled.

*   *   *

After that nigga spent a few bands we went back to his crib so that Zy and Mackie could have some alone time. I knew that the shit with Kia was still bothering her and so she needed her man to confirm that she was his number one. Bitches like Kia came a dime a dozen. They wanted a nigga for what he had to offer. I was that chick too in a way, but I knew how those types of relationships played out. A bitch was either going to love a nigga, or use him for his ends. It was impossible to do both. Most bitches don't realize that they love a nigga that they call themselves using until it's over. Usually when a bitch was using a nigga he was using her for something too. Typically that was for sex. A dude like Zy would never stay with a chick like that. He was meant to be with a good girl like Mackie, because he was a thug with a heart.

Unlike that dumb ass bitch Kia, I knew how to let go when shit was over. What I did was move on to the next nigga with paper, because that was my thing. Love never came into play because I knew better. That bitch Kia was trying to be an opportunist, but obviously she'd caught feelings for her sponsor. A real woman knew how to get her coins from a nigga and keep it cute if he wanted to act an ass. Fuck that nigga if he wanted another bitch. What I did was make that nigga forget his new bitch every time he saw me. That new bitch would never compare to me, so instead of fighting bitches with my fists, I fought them by making it so that their man still wanted me when it was over and done with. That was why I dared that bitch to put her hands on my best friend one more damn time. It was so clear that she wasn't a bitch of my caliber or Mackie's because Zy did not want her ass. He was so in love with Mackie that he didn't even see Kia's hoe ass at all.

Anyway, that was that and I was ready to see what all the hype was about. Cane swore up and down that his head was a beast and I wanted to know firsthand. Fuck all the damn talking.

We were chilling in his living room on the sofa smoking a blunt when he started the nasty talk again. Bags from Coach, Michael Kors, True Religion and Ralph Lauren were on the floor beneath our feet. That nigga was so busy putting his hands on my ass that he couldn't even carry my bags any further.

"Damn, I want all that ass in my fuckin' face while I eat that pussy out from the back. I ain't even the type of nigga who be passin' out head and shit." He licked his lips and his gray eyes were stuck on me as he did.

"That shit's sexy as fuck?"

"What?" He inched closer to me and started kissing my neck.

"Mmm, the way you were lickin' your lips and those pretty ass eyes."

"Let me lick yo' pussy like that while I stare you down wit' these eyes. Now that'll be some sexy shit."

I wanted some cash too, so, it was time to turn the seduction way the fuck up.

"After you lick this pussy you gon' want to put your dick up in it right?" I gave him one of my sexiest looks as I bit my bottom lip.

"Hell yeah, what the fuck you think. I wanna eat it and I wanna feel the bottom of that mufucka."

"Mmmm," I moaned because he was still kissing and sucking gently on my neck. "That's my spot…"

His hands were inside of my panties and my pussy was already wet. Shit, I think I'd been wet since I first saw his ass the day before.

"If I let you put your dick up in this good pussy, what you gon' give me?" I licked my lips as I stared up at him. My long lashes were low and I knew that made my sexy ass eyes look even sexier. That nigga was under my spell.

"Damn, I'm gon' give you this good dick and you gon' nut…"

I moved away from his kisses and flashed him a smirk. "Other than the dick…"

He looked at me and shook his head. "What you want shawty? We just went to Phipps like you asked and... shit, I'on even be spendin' money on no hoes like that."

"Maybe because those hoes weren't as fiyah in the bedroom as me." My voice was low and sexy.

That made him raise an eyebrow. "Damn," he whispered as I stood up and slowly took off everything except for my silver stiletto heel Gucci pumps.

"Leave those on shawty." His eyes were big as hell as he stared at me with his tongue literally hanging out of his mouth. "Mmm, turn around and let me see that fat ass."

I put my hand out and then put my left leg over his shoulder. "You wouldn't want me to not have any spendin' cash while I'm here right? I mean, for the next two weeks while I'm here, you gon' want to keep gettin' this pussy. I promise you. Make it worth my while."

That nigga's eyes were glued to the nice, plump, hairless treasure between my legs as he reached in his pocket for his bill fold. He counted off ten one hundred dollar bills and tried to pass them to me. I grabbed the bill fold instead and took the larger stack of money out of it. I gave him the bill fold back and he shook his head as he put the ten hundreds back in his pocket. I figured that I had at least three g's

"That should do for now."

"You somethin' else ma," he said with eyes that were glazed over with lust.

"Shut up and eat this pussy nigga. Ain't that what you been beggin' for all day?"

*   *   *

Damn, Cane had turned the tables on my shit talking ass. That nigga's dick wasn't even the longest I'd ever had. It was probably seven and a half, maybe eight inches, but it was thicker than my arm. I thought I was going to whip his ass, but he had me screaming and clawing at the walls and shit. Okay, the head was already off the chain. That nigga had literally ate me from the sofa to the bed. When he pulled me to the edge of his king sized bed and told me to bend over, he did all types of shit with his tongue from the crack of my ass to my clit and back again. My first thought was that nigga had a wack dick game because he had perfected the art of pussy eating.

Boy was a bitch wrong for the first time in my life. Well, maybe the second time. Anyway, that nigga was dicking me down and I was trying my best not to show it. I was throwing it back and shit, but he was making me feel like I could keep fucking him and get to know him at the same damn time. Shit, he must've had me fucked up to be thinking about doing more than spending his money.

"Damn…fuck…Cane…shit…" I knew that we'd been fucking for at least twenty minutes and I was used to my good pussy making a nigga bust already.

"Mmm, this shit is…good as hell," he groaned as he worked me over from the back.

We'd started out with him on top with my legs behind my head, but of course he wanted to see all that ass in motion.

"I know it's good, but…in that case…why you ain't cum yet?" Maybe I was just used to niggas not giving a fuck if I got mine before them.

"Shit…I'on know who you been fuckin' …but…a real nigga take his time to enjoy good pussy. Why rush it? I'm a grown ass man. I can hold…damn…my nut for you to cum first. If the pussy was wack I'd be tryna get out this mufuka. Shit, I ain't tryna do nothin' but keep strokin'."

"I did cum though," I admitted. Normally I didn't cum that often, but he'd damn sure made it happen early in the game.

"One time ain't enough. I want you to cum again...right now! Cum for me...wit' that fat ass!" He smacked both of my ass cheeks and then he really started grinding up in it all good.

"Mmm...damn..." I had to bite the pillow and shit to keep from screaming.

That nigga had my shit pulsating because he was really moving his ass like a snake and shit. Most niggas was just with that in and out shit, but he had a nice grind with it that was making me nut over and over again. I wasn't used to that shit, but it damn sure felt good as hell. Not only had I got a shopping spree and some money, but I'd actually enjoyed the sex. Hmmm.

"You cumin'?" He asked lifting up to go deeper.

When he gave me all the dick and then started going in in deep circles I was cuming hard as hell.

"Fuck yeah!" I screamed as he held on to my waist without letting up on that deep, slow grind. "Cane....shiiiiiiiiiiiiiiiiiiiit! "

"You wanna cum again?" He asked as he spread my ass cheeks. "Damn, I'm crazy over this mufucka already."

My legs trembled. "I can't…mmm…cum again…"

He leaned over to kiss my neck and then my back. My body shivered as I twerked all over that good ass dick.

"Sure you can sexy…that's what that pussy's made for. It was meant to cum and shit."

He was right because in less than a second my abdomen tightened and I was cuming again from the dick alone. That nigga wasn't even touching my clit. What the fuck? How did he do that? It had been done before, but not the way he was doing it. It was just something about the way *he* was fucking doing it. Then he had the nerve to keep those sexy ass eyes on me. I loved the way he looked at me. It was like he was amazed or something. Well, I wasn't surprised. I did have that million dollar pussy.

"Damn…Cane…" I looked back at him. "You…mmm…got some good ass dick nigga. For real." I meant that shit.

He really started showing off then by going long and deep. I could tell that he couldn't hold out any longer. That platinum shit was too much for his ass. That nigga had found his match in the bed. Shit. I ain't play no games.

"Fuck…ahhhh….shit!!!!" He held on to me tight as hell as his body jerked and shook. "Damn…that pussy got some grip."

Then he pulled out and kissed my neck.

"You got some fiyah ass pussy just like you said shawty. Plus, I can't understand how a woman your size got such a fat ass. You sure you ain't pay for that shit." He squeezed my ass cheeks and then kissed each one of them.

I laughed. "Hell nah nigga. That's all me.'

He smacked my ass and stood up. "It's mine now shawty. Bet that. I ain't gon' lie though. If I ain't have this damn condom on, I'on know. You was puttin' the walls down on a nigga. Damn."

He went into the bathroom to wash up and I went in after him. I wasn't really prepared for it, but he actually cuddled with me and shit. I hoped that nigga didn't think he was claiming me because he'd spent some money and got some ass. Hmmm. He just didn't know me. It was kind of weird at first, but all of the orgasms I had made me tired as hell, so I was out like a light in no time.

Chapter 8

Cane

At first shawty's ass had me in a trance and then the pussy on her had me in a daze for a minute. She had a snapper. That was that super good, tight ass pussy that securely wrapped around and squeezed the hell out of a nigga's dick. Once I got in that shit it was like a vacuum seal that locked my dick in place. I'd never had no pussy like that before. When it was all said and done though, she was the total package. Yeah, the physical had always done it for a nigga like me, but Beyanka was wild and feisty like I liked. Baby girl was a challenge and that was what I needed. Yeah, she was the type of chick who could finally tame a nigga like me, but I had to get in her head. I had to see if she was really the type of chick I thought she was.

Clearly she was the type who got what she could out of a nigga, but she'd never fucked with a nigga like me. There was a match out there for everybody and something was making me think that shawty was mine. Before I let some good pussy and a fat ass cloud my vision, I had to see if I was thinking clearly. It was time to feel lil' mama out and see where her head was at for real.

We'd been chilling around the crib all day eating, drinking, smoking and fucking. It was like we couldn't keep our hands off each other. The physical attraction between us was stronger than a mufucka. It was like she was a flame and I was the moth and shit. That shit was crazy as hell, but a nigga was enjoying that shit. Beyanka was a fire cracker and the more time I spent with her, the more I was into her ass.

"Damn, so you mean to tell me that you think the Lakers are the best team in NBA history?" I asked in disbelief.

"Hell yeah," she said matter of factily. "Dr. J., Magic Johnson, Kobe fuckin' Bryant nigga. Stop playin'."

I passed her the blunt and shook my head. "Hell nah. I gotta disagree. I gotta give it to the Chicago Bulls when they had Michael Jordan and Scottie Pippen dustin' mufuckas off the court and shit."

She took a pull and laid back against the cushions of the sofa. "Nigga bye. You must be fucked up right now. Is it my pussy or the weed?"

"Both," I said seriously as I pulled her shirt up to reveal her pretty, perky B cup breasts.

It was crazy how mami's titties weren't all that big and she had that itty bitty waist, but her hips and ass blossomed out like a flower in bloom. Her legs were nice and thick too. Damn, I loved her figure. I was more of an ass man than a breast man anyway and the titties she had were enough for me. Besides, she had some big, suckable ass nipples. Shit, I didn't want her to go back to VA.

She laughed and blew smoke out of her nose. "So, I must've backed up the shit I was talkin'."

"Damn right. I ain't even been answerin' my damn phone and shit knowin' I got business to handle."

In a short amount of time I had learned a lot about her. She was an open book and I liked that shit. It was like mami had no secrets. She even let me in on how she was thinking about robbing a nigga. That shit made me laugh although I knew that shawty was on some real ass street shit. It was all good being that she wasn't going to act on that craziness.

"I'm really feelin' you right now Cane. I'on know if it's just for the moment or not. It's no tellin' what's gon' happen between us. All I know is right now I'm enjoyin' it, so let's just chill and see what's it's gon' be. Shit, I gotta go back to VA soon and I don't really do relationships, especially not long distance ones."

I nodded as she passed me the blunt. "It is what it is. You sexy and you fun as hell. I ain't tryna wife you up or nothin', but I ain't tryna share you while you here either. While you here, you belong to me. When you go back to VA the rest is up to yo' fine ass."

"Hmm, a'ight then. I guess that's fair."

I took a pull of the blunt as my phone vibrated on the coffee table. It was Zy and I figured he was calling because Mackie had tried to call Bey. It was after three pm and neither of us was trying to talk to anybody.

"Hello," I answered to put her home girl's mind at ease.

"Nigga, damn. You can't answer the fuckin' phone. I know you feelin' old girl and shit, but it ain't no vacay. The grind don't stop 'cause you want a pussy break nigga."

I sighed. "I'm 'bout to make sure them Charlotte niggas straight mufucka. Calm the fuck down. Shit is handled already."

"Better be. A'ight nigga. Do what you gotta do, but make sure them niggas on point. I ain't got time for no bullshit right now man."

"Already nigga. I'll holla..."

"Baby said where her girl at?"

"Right here nigga."

"Should've known. She good right? I'm only askin' 'cuz shorty wanna know. Not 'cuz I think you'd do something man," Zy said.

"Say something so your girl'll know you good shawty." I passed Beyanka the phone.

"I'm good Mackie. You know that. Stop bein' all motherly and shit. You know how I do," Bey said jokingly. "Bye bitch. I'm 'bout to suck this nigga's dick real quick."

I hung up the phone and closed my eyes when she wrapped her lips around my hardness.

"Mmm..." She was slurping and devouring my dick so good. I couldn't help but lean my head back against the sofa cushion with the blunt between my lips and enjoy the way that shit looked and felt. "Dayum..."

*　　　*　　　*

Beyanka agreed to stay at my crib and wait for me while I handled shit at the traps and on the blocks for that nigga Zy. It was up to me to make sure that the twenty keys made it to Charlotte and that all the spots had been replenished. I was at the top ranks of the Cues, but I wasn't at the point where I could keep my hands clean yet.

It was kind of fucked up being that I was the one who had put Zy on and shit. I had no idea that Diablo was his pops at first, but when he passed me in the ranks it was no surprise. Honestly, I felt some type of way about it. I'd been a Cue since I was eleven and at the age of twenty I'd put in way more work than that nigga Zy had. Still, after only three years of duty that mufucka was on top.

That nigga was cool otherwise and up until that moment I had no animosity toward him. Bey was a bad ass bitch and if it was up to me she would stay right there in the A with me. Fuck letting her go back to VA. I had to just sit back for the moment and let Zyon build his empire. When the time came I'd plot my take over with my bad, big booty bitch by my side. Mmm, that would be the shit. Mackie just wasn't built to reign beside a boss. She was pretty and shit, but she was too timid. A boss needed a bitch who was going to bust her guns with him. A boss needed a bitch who was going to make sure that no nigga ever rose above him in the streets. In Bey, I'd found a boss bitch and I knew that shit.

Mackie and Beyanka were best friends, but I knew how much Mackie loved those dollars. If I played my cards right her loyalty would be with me and me alone. I mean, I wasn't planning to do anything to that nigga Zy.

Shit, his pops was like a living legend in the streets. It would be crazy of me to try him. I just knew that I had to make my own name no matter how I did it. I lived for money and bitches and in order to have one, you had to have the other. When I looked at Bey I thought of ways she could help a nigga make more money. If I couldn't be the leader of the Cues, I had to do something else to make the streets remember me.

"What you thinkin' 'bout nigga?" Deniro asked as I took the huge duffel bag of money from him.

"This money nigga. What you thinkin' bout?"

He laughed mockingly. "Hmm. Zy told me how you been all stuck to Mackie's friend's ass and shit. You rushin' and shit to get back to her? Let me find out you all in love wit' that hoe already."

"Nigga fuck you! Just make sure them niggas on the way back from Charlotte and shit!"

*   *   *

I was back up in Bey's good ass pussy when she decided she wanted to record that shit.

"Hold the phone for me baby. Your view is better than mine," she said breathlessly.

"Oh, so you gon' watch this when you leave me huh?" I asked stroking that thang good.

She moaned and sucked my pointer finger. "Mmm hmm, I'm gon' watch it and play in my pussy."

"Damn, make sure you record that shit and send it to me. Mmm."

We'd only stopped messing around long enough to eat, because like I said before, I couldn't get enough of that shit. According to her, she'd be gone in a week and some change, so I was trying to get all of that I could before then. It wasn't everyday that a nigga came across pussy that damn good. I'd been with maybe a hundred women, but that good shit between her legs was one in a million.

"Mmm...work that shit mami...damn!" I groaned as she grinded those crazy ass pussy muscles on top of me.

Just when a nigga's nuts starting tingling and I was holding on to that ass ready to let loose, I heard the loud sound of glass breaking.

"Cum for me daddy," Bey coaxed me sexily just as I was about to ask if she heard that shit.

I held on to her juicy ass cheeks and closed my eyes as she milked my dick to an amazing orgasm.

"Ahhhh...fuck..." All I could do was grip her soft body as I rode that shit out. It felt so good that I was about to ignore it when I heard the crashing sound again.

"What the hell?" Bey asked with a frown on her face.

After she lifted her body up from mine, I got up to look out of the window. It was a chick I was fucking with named Ne Ne standing on the hood of my car busting the windshield out with a bat. She was swinging that shit like a mad woman.

"Ah...shit!" I yelled before pulling my boxers and jeans on.

"Who the fuck is that bitch?" Bey asked as she got dressed too.

"Don't worry 'bout it ma. Just some hoe I was fuckin'." I was out of breath as I thought about that bitch fucking up my brand new, cocaine white, big body Benz.

"Oh really?" She asked with a smile on her face.

Uh oh. I knew what that smile meant. Bey was wild as hell, so she wanted to start some shit. I already knew that the neighbors had probably called the cops.

When I was at my spot in the hood, I acted accordingly, but Ne Ne had brought that hood shit to the suburbs. She was tripping because I hadn't been checking for her since I met Bey. We weren't together like that, but I guess that good dick had her in her feelings.

"Look Bey, shit is already out of hand wit' that hoe bein' that she's tearin' up my shit. You stay right here," I told her as I rushed out of the front door.

"Bitch! What the fuck you think you doin'! I'm gon' whoop your fuckin' ass if you don't get off my car and get the fuck up outta here!" I yelled as I made my way over to her.

Now, I wasn't one to just be beating up on no females, but that bitch was asking for it.

"Come get me off your fuckin' car nigga!" She yelled as she busted the passenger side window out next. "If I could'a got inside your house I would've beat yo' ass wit' this fuckin' bat muthafucka!"

Ne Ne was a cute, light brown skinned honey with curly hair who reminded me of a younger version of Tracy Elise Ross. She didn't have all that ass back there though. Her shape was nice, but Bey's body was killing hers hands down.

I tried to calm down before she did anymore damage to my whip. As I ran my hand over my face, she kept bashing the windows out of my shit.

"Look Ne Ne, calm down yo'. That shit you doin' right now ain't even necessary…"

"Oh, it's necessary nigga! You already knew that if you fucked me over this was gonna happen! I told yo' light bright, wanna be gangsta ass that I was gonna come to your cracker ass neighborhood and show out if you ever gave me your ass to kiss! Didn't I?" She had stopped swinging the bat and put her other hand on her hips to wait for my response.

She had told me that, but I didn't give a fuck. Her stupid ass warning didn't mean a damn thing because I'd never agreed to be her man and shit. That bitch was delusional as hell and it was the first time I hoped to see the fucking cops, because for once I hadn't done shit. She was the one tearing my shit up. Although I didn't want the police lurking around, I didn't give a damn at that point being that I didn't do dirt where I laid my head.

"I don't really give a shit about all that yo'. You might be pissed that a nigga ain't got at you in a few days, but you ain't my girl shawty. Take that shit for what it was and bounce off my whip wit' it. Damn." I shook my head as she started swinging that damn bat again, denting up the hood of my car.

A nigga was just about to grab that bitch and drag her off my Benz when I heard the sound of glass breaking elsewhere. When I looked up Bey was using a crowbar that she'd found in my garage to bust the headlights on Ne Ne's silver Range Rover.

"What the fuck! I'm gon' kill you bitch!" Ne Ne yelled as she finally climbed down from the hood of my car.

I quickly rushed over to Bey because I knew that shit was about to go down. Ne Ne had a bat and she had a crowbar in her hand. There was no way I could allow them to beat each other down in front of my crib. Hell nah. Now, that was heat I did not need coming down on me.

"Bey, damn, I told you to stay in the house yo'." I was scared that she would hit me if I got too close to her ass.

"Fuck that! You wasn't convincin' the bitch to get off yo' whip wit' that bullshit you was talkin'. She's off your shit now right?" Bey was standing there holding that iron crowbar in her hand like she was about to knock somebody's block off.

Ne Ne was right behind me, but I managed to block her path from Bey before attempting to grab her bat.

"Go back in the house yo'," I said all out of breath. Damn, I smoked too much.

"I'm gonna go in the house after I do this…" She pulled out a switch blade from the pocket of her jeans and held on to the crowbar with her other hand.

"I'm gon' kill you bitch! You better not scratch up my muthafuckin' truck!"

She was fighting hard as hell to get away from me, but a nigga was too damn strong for her ass. Bey stood right there and carved something in the side of Ne Ne's ride. I didn't know what it said, but I could imagine because it took long enough.

"You wanna kill me bitch?" Bey taunted and pointed the knife at her with an evil little smirk on her pretty face. "Well, I'll be here for another week or so. If you wanna find me, I'll be right here fuckin' the dick you out here actin' all crazy over. If you had played your cards right we could've had a threesome and enjoyed that shit together. I'm a lover, not a fighter, but you pushed me bitch." She flicked her tongue at her as she put the blade down and put it back in her pocket.

"Bitch! I swear on my fuckin' life! Let me go Cane!" She was biting and scratching me and everything.

"Shit, go in the house Bey!" I yelled over my shoulder. "For real yo'!"

"Fuck this shit! I'll beat yo' hoe ass later since he won't let me do it now!" Bey said menacingly as she headed toward the house.

The low wails of sirens in the distance let me know that somebody had called the police just like I thought they would.

"So, that's what you been doin' huh?" Ne Ne yelled spitting all in my face. "That fuckin' weaved out, ass injection lookin' ass hoe!"

Bey stopped dead in her tracks. "What? For real?" She asked making her way back over to us.

I shook my head. "Just go back in the house Bey. The cop's comin' yo. Go inside."

Damn old girl was a hot head, shit.

"Nah, that bitch wanna talk her way into that ass whoppin' right now I see!" Bey swung that crowbar and my instinct caused me to move Ne Ne out of the way since I was still holding her.

True, she had busted the windows out of my Benz, but Bey was aiming for her face. I didn't want shit to get that ugly and out of hand in front of my house. The crowbar hit me hard as hell in my back instead, but I was a man and I could take the pain. It hurt like hell though and I could only imagine what it would've done to Ne Ne's face.

At that point I realized that all I could do was try to get Ne Ne's crazy ass in her ride, so that mess would be over. I'd managed to take her bat away and it had rolled somewhere. I was just hoping that Bey would calm the fuck down before the cops got there, or she was going to get locked up.

"I'm not gonna tell you again Bey! Go in the fuckin' crib!" I barked angrily.

She finally took me seriously and walked toward the house again talking shit under her breath. That time she went inside.

"Ohhhh, I'm gon' get you and that bitch Cane! How you gon' fuckin' play me out over that tired ass lookin' hoe! Huh? Nigga, I…"

"Shut the fuck up and get the hell outta here Ne Ne shit! Do your crazy ass wanna go to jail! Huh!

Out here actin' like this over some dick that ain't even yours and ain't never been yours!"

When I saw the police lights in the distance, I immediately let her go. "You can leave or you can stay here and explain to them why my windows busted out of my ride and shit."

"And I can tell them how that bitch busted my headlights and scratched my whip!" She yelled back.

"Well, I'm only bailin' her out! Make your choice bitch!" My face was stone cold and she knew that I'd let her ass sit there and rot in jail.

She was just another gold digger in the hood who liked to flex, but really didn't have shit. Her pussy and head game got her a Range and a nice condo, but she couldn't maintain that shit on her own. That was why she had to try and hold on to a baller like me. I hadn't really given that bitch too much. Just some gas money or maybe a bill paid. Every now and then I'd get her hair or nails done, but that was it. She was just something to do, but not something I wanted to continue doing.

"Fuck you nigga and that dog ass lookin' hoe you fuckin'! I'm still gon' kill that bitch when I see her!" She stomped off to her Range, got in and drove off in the opposite direction screeching tires.

I still didn't see what Bey had scratched on the side of the car. Before the police pulled up, I rushed back into the house with the bat that Ne Ne had. If it was up to me I wasn't even going to the door for those bitches.

"Damnit Bey!" I yelled furiously when I made it around the corner to the living room where she was standing.

"What? Damn, at least I didn't hit or cut that bitch. It could've been worse." She had a look on her face like she didn't know why I was pissed off. "Shit, she was fuckin' yo' shit up. You must like that ugly big nose hoe."

Ne Ne was pretty, but she did have a long nose. I had to laugh. "I don't like her like that. It was a fuck thing and that's it."

"Mmm hmm…"

"So, what did you scratch into her car?" I was curious to know.

"Big Bird lookin bitch," she said with a sly grin.

I couldn't help but die laughing.

"Everything light skinned ain't cute nigga," she added.

"Right," I agreed.

The sound of a knock at the door cut off our temporary amusement.

"Police! Open up!"

"Go in the back. I'm just gon' tell them that I had an argument with my ex and I don't wanna press charges." I figured it was best to tell them something.

She nodded and went into the guest bedroom in the back. All I could do was shake my head as I walked over to the door to smooth shit over with the cops. I knew they would have their suspicions about a young black man with a nice crib in a gated community with luxury vehicles, but they didn't have shit on me. That was not the way I envisioned my evening after getting some helluva pussy, but hey that was just how real shit got when you had that dick game mastered.

Chapter 9

Mackie

My mother had just called to tell me that she was back at Tre and Princess's. I was ready to go ahead and face the music although I was nervous as hell. Sylvia Braswell was a hard ass woman and that was the reason I'd taken the straight and narrow road for so long. I couldn't say that I actually wanted to be so damn disciplined.

I had called Beyanka to see why she still wasn't at Zy's yet so she could accompany me like she said she would. It was a good thing my eye had lightened and the swelling was gone. Now it was easier to cover with makeup. That was one less thing for my mother to fuss about.

"Hello," she answered. I could hear some loud ass music playing in the background.

"Bey, where you at? I called you over an hour ago."

Zy was sitting there on the sofa patiently waiting. I loved how he never rushed me or acted like I was getting on his nerves. I blew him a kiss and he pretended to catch it.

Suddenly the music had stopped and I could hear her clearly.

"I'm so sorry boo. Cane ended up gettin' me a last minute sew in appointment with his cousin. You know I need my hair done girl," she said. I could hear her patting herself in the head all hard like it was itching something serious.

"Well, by the way you beatin' your scalp I believe you." I rolled my eyes at how superficial my best friend could be.

She'd promised to be there when I talked to my mother, but she was more concerned about a damn sew in.

"I'm sorry Mackie. I had to get in when she could fit me in. I can't be 'round here lookin' like a hot mess girl. You know I got your back, so if your moms start trippin' just call me. K," she said sounding all happy and shit.

She'd told me about that chick Ne Ne and their confrontation. So we both suddenly had beef with a hoe. Damn, some women were just too damn thirsty for a man's attention.

"Yeah, whatever. I'll call you later." I was disappointed that I'd be facing my mom alone.

When I hung up Zy gave me a sympathetic look.

"Do you want me to talk to your mom with you 'cause…"

I killed that noise real quick. "Hell no. I'll handle my mother alone. Let's just go, so I can get that shit over with."

*   *   *

"How the hell can your new boyfriend afford to buy you a car like that? Huh? How old is he? You got a sugar dady?" My mother narrowed her eyes at me accusingly.

"No ma," I sighed. "Do you remember the guy who was with Tre's friend Diablo at the hospital that day? He's Diablo's son Zyon."

My mother put her hands on her hips and her mouth formed into an O like she was surprised that I was talking about him. She took a deep breath and then started pacing the floor. I knew that was a bad sign. She was pissed.

"I know you ain't talkin' 'bout that lil' nigga that I saw with his pants saggin' off his ass and those huge diamonds in his ears? Unt uhh. Not that lil' mufucka with all those tattoos on his neck and I think I saw one on his face…"

"He does not have a tattoo on his face ma," I said rolling my eyes.

"Give him that damn car back!" She demanded.

"He won't take it back."

"What? He's a gang banger or something? How old is he? How the hell did he get you a car like that? I know all about Diablo and what he and your cousin used to do and shit!"

"He's eighteen and…"

"Eighteen!" My mother was livid and I could tell that she wanted to wrap her fingers around my neck and squeeze some sense into me. "Don't you stand here and tell me that he don't run with the Cues. If his damn daddy did it he's doin' it too! Right? That's how he got you that car huh? I know all about lil' punk ass niggas like him. I've been tellin' you the scoop about them all your life and that's who you choose to fall for. You're at a crossroad in your life where you can't let nothin' make you lose focus! What the hell is wrong with you? You gon' throw away all you worked so hard for!" There were tears in her eyes and I knew that I was hurting her for the first time in my life.

She had changed her life for me and I knew that she expected me to be perfect for that reason, but I wasn't. I needed to make my own mistakes and she needed to realize that my life was not hers.

"I'm sorry mama. I'm not trying to throw anything away. I love him and he gave me the car so I'd be able to get to and from school. He doesn't want me to be on the bus or train because it can be unsafe." I tried to reason with my mother, but she had her eyes closed like she was trying to keep from snapping on me.

"Bein' with his ass is unsafe! You think you love him Mackenzie, but you don't know what love is! You're only nineteen lil' girl! You don't know shit! Wake the hell up! That lil' horny ass toad is just after one thing! That car and all the shit he's gonna buy you is to get in your fuckin' drawers, but I'm sure he's already done that! What? He tickled that spot huh? Made you cum! You ain't never felt nothing like that have you? You ain't in love! Your lil' ass is just dicmitized! Well your mama's been there and believe me, that ain't shit! That shit gets old real fast and he'll be on to the next lil' fast ass hot tamale that he sees!"

I shook my head because I couldn't believe her. "No, this is not like that! It's deeper than sex with him!

You can't compare me to yourself and what you did. I'm not you! Daddy didn't leave you for anybody mama. He was murdered. You don't know if he would've been..."

"I know what kinda man your daddy was lil' girl! He wasn't shit, just like most men!"

At that point Tre and Princess had come downstairs to intervene.

"Look Sylvia, I know that you're pissed, but could you two please hold it down. The twins are asleep..." Princess said pleading with her green eyes.

"Whatever!" My mother snapped. "How could you two allow my daughter to be runnin' around with some damn street thug?"

Tre spoke up. "Zy's a good kid Sylvia. You should be the last one to judge, damn, you love me like I'm your brother. Don't forget the shit you..." His milk chocolate toned face was all screwed up when she interrupted him.

"I'm your aunt Tre, so don't bring up shit I did! I don't keep shit from Mackie! I've taught her to learn from me!"

"But mama, I have to learn for myself. Don't you get it? I'm not a little girl anymore." I tried my best to level with her, but she was only seeing things her way.

"That's true Sylvia. I mean, Mackie is an adult now and she has to make her own decisions when it comes to who she loves," Princess spoke up on my behalf.

My mother sighed and threw her hands up. "Three against one I see. What the fuck would you two do if Naveah walked up in here with some street nigga with his pants off his ass and tattoos every fuckin' where? What then?"

"This ain't about us or Naveah. It's about the fact that you seem to have forgotten your past woman," Tre said looking shocked. "You loved who you wanted to love when you were her age. You ain't met the nigga and you think you got him all figured out."

"Look mama, you can talk to Bey. She met him and..."

My mother looked at me like she had turned into the devil in the flesh. Her eyes were damn near scary. "Fuck that little hoe! I don't wanna hear nothin' she gotta say. She probably wanna fuck your lil' so called boyfriend!"

"What? Are you serious? Don't talk about my friend like that!" I was so mad I could hit my own damn mama at that point. I thought she liked Beyanka.

"I'm done with this," Princess said and walked back upstairs.

"C'mon Sylvia, don't be so hard on her. Let her live her own life. She's done everything you wanted in the order that you wanted. Give her some space and let her grow up man," Tre said trying to make her try to see things my way, but it was no use.

"You made your choice huh?" My mother asked as she shook her head at me.

"What choice mama? I want to be with him, but don't make me choose between you two. That is so wrong." Tears filled my eyes and spilled down my cheeks.

"I found a house in Stone Mountain, but if you decide to be with him you're not welcome there. You'll no longer be a part of my life!"

I couldn't believe she had taken it there. I'd moved to Atlanta for her and she was turning her back on me. Why the hell did she think it was okay for her to turn her back on her own daughter? Just because I'd made one decision out of a million that she didn't agree with. At that moment I hated her.

"Really ma? Just because I love somebody that you don't want me to love? Just because I won't bow down to you like I always do! You know what! I don't need you then! Thank you for letting me stay here Tre." I grabbed my purse, walked out and slammed the door behind me.

My eyes were blurred with tears as I walked to my car. When I got in, I could barely see, so I calmed down and wiped my eyes before dialing Zy's number.

"How did it go?" He asked without even saying hello.

At the sound of his voice my tears started all over again. "She's done with me Zy! My mama hates me!" I wailed. "She doesn't understand how I feel about you and she won't even try."

"Baby, calm down okay, I can't understand you. Where are you?" He asked.

I took a breath and wiped my eyes again. "I'm in the car on my way to you. I'll explain everything when I get there."

"Okay," he said. "But promise me that you won't be cryin' and shit. I don't wanna have to worry about you not bein' able to drive. If you need me to I'll come get you."

That was a bad idea, so I assured him that I was okay to drive. "I'm fine baby. I promise. I'll see you in a few okay."

"Okay," he said and hung up.

I thought about calling Bey, but decided not to. All I wanted was to be with Zy and for him to wrap his strong arms around me. The only thing I longed for was the scent of his cologne and the way his soft lips felt on mine. Damn, I realized that I was in love for the first time in my life. That was something that most people didn't get to experience for real and I was one of the lucky ones. Why would I throw that away? I loved my mother and I prayed that she would come around one day. Zy was the man that I loved and I wasn't going to leave him alone. Not for my mother, not for Kia, not for any damn body.

*   *   *

Zyon

"You can stay right here wit' me sexy. I would love that shit."

I was wrapped up in Zy's arms right where I wanted to be more than anything in the world. When I showed up at the door, he didn't say a word. All he did was pick me up and carry me straight to the bed where we made sweet, sweaty love until I came so hard that nothing else mattered other than that moment.

After the tingles subsided reality had set in and I told him all about my argument with my mom. He played in my hair as I told him all about how she'd practically written me off because I loved him.

"We haven't been together long enough to be living together. I think I should get my own place. I'm gonna get the job at Verizon and move into…"

"Okay. If you don't wanna live together yet I'll get you a spot that's not far from campus. That way…"

"Zy, can I do something on my own…please. I don't want to feel like you're going to try to fix everything. I'm not helpless," I said feeling so frustrated with him and my mother.

It felt like they were both trying to control me.

"So, you still think I'm tryna control you? The problem is that you won't let me help you. You see it as me controllin' you, but you're just afraid to lose control. That shit ain't about me. That's all on you. Nothin' I do for you is about control Mackie. It's about love, but you're too damn bull headed to see that shit."

It was clear that I called her Mackie instead of Baby when she pissed me off.

She sighed. "Okay. If I let you get me a place I am going to pay my own bills when I start working."

I shook my head. "Nah. You can work if you want, but I'm payin' your bills woman. My woman don't pay bills. End of discussion."

She opened her mouth to protest, but I used my tongue to trace a hot trail from her belly button to her clit. There was silence, but I knew that wouldn't last long. Her breathing became labored as I started to gently suck on her love button. That was what she called it and I thought that shit was so cute.

"Mmm…damn…you know how to shut me up." She grabbed the top of my head and held on as I took her away on another orgasmic trip.

I sure did know how to shut her up. True, it wasn't going to fix things, but it was definitely going to take her mind off them for a little while.

*　　*　　*

Her warm body was beneath mine and she felt so good, but she was clenching the shit out of my dick. That was not in a good way either. Baby seemed distracted and I noticed that when we made love she seemed to not always be there mentally. So, I stopped and reluctantly lifted myself from her tight, warm wetness.

"What's wrong?" She asked planting kisses on my face. "Why'd you stop?"

"C'mere," I said as I pulled her up from the bed and led her into the master bath.

There was a full length mirror on the back of the door and so I closed it so that she could see herself. I stood behind her and slowly swept her hair away from her neck.

"I want you to take a good look at yourself," I said as I stared lovingly at the beauty that was in front of me.

She looked away from the mirror and sucked her teeth. "You stopped fucking me so I could look in the mirror? Was it that bad Zy? What man stops in the middle of sex if it's good?"

"See, that's your problem right there. You sound all insecure and shit when you ain't got a reason to be. You're fuckin' gorgeous. Look at your eyes and your lips. That's what caught my attention at first. There's so much pain in your eyes and I wanted to make it go away. Your lips made me wanna kiss you so bad and that's why I did it at Daren and Reco's reception."

I traced my fingers softly from her neck to her breasts. "You're perfect Baby. Maybe not in your eyes, but all I see is perfection. I know that they say nobody's perfect, but you're perfect for me." When I kissed her neck I could tell that I had her full attention.

She closed her eyes.

"Open your eyes."

She did.

I let my fingers brush against the flesh of her beautiful pussy and then her thighs. "You open these for me, but you won't open you mind."

A look of curiosity showed in her eyes, so I explained.

"When I'm inside you, you won't open up for me. You won't let go and when a woman won't let go, her body can't relax. Your pussy's hella tight and I love that shit, I do. I love makin' love to you. It's just that you clench up and won't take *all* the dick."

"Well it damn sure feels like I be taking it all. What do you mean Zy?" She rolled her eyes at me like I'd hurt her feelings or something.

"Baby damn, it ain't like I said your pussy ain't no good. I'm just sayin' I want you to let everything go. Don't think about Kia, your mama, or your past. I want you to focus on the love you feel for me when I'm inside you. If you do that you'll open up for me and you'll enjoy makin' love so much better. It's just one more example of how afraid you are of losin' control. Give me your body and your mind and I promise I'll take you to heights of pleasure that you never knew were possible. Don't get mad when I tell you this, okay."

She nodded as my fingers continued to caress her skin gently. I was hoping to awaken all of the nerve endings in her body and increase the blood flow to her pussy. That way when I was up in it again, she'd relax her muscles and let me go deep. All I wanted was to be deep inside my baby, but she was making sure that I only went as far as she'd let me go.

"I've been wit' a few older women and I notice that although they can control their pussy muscles, or may feel tight to me, I'm able to go in as deep as I want to. That's because they are more secure with themselves and their bodies. They're old enough to know that there is nothing wrong wit' enjoyin' sex, so they're able to relax. See, you're still under your mother's influence. She's told you for so long that sex is wrong and it's unnatural unless you're married. Well, if you're married to a doctor or lawyer. Shit, do you really think your mama always thought that?" I chuckled sarcastically as my fingers gently parted her pussy lips.

"No," she whispered just as my fingers met her moist, warm opening.

"You wouldn't be here if she did. Anyway, you're not as experienced as those women and I know that. I'm just tellin' you that if you let go, I can give you the two inches of dick that you won't let me put in you. Don't get me wrong ma, I love the tightness, but if you open that thing up and then hold a nigga in, mmm..." I shook my head and thought about how good that shit would feel.

"I understand what you're sayin' baby. You're right. I do find myself clenching up and shit because you're big baby and it hurts sometimes."

I kissed her cheek and then sucked gently on her earlobe. "If you relax your muscles it won't hurt. See, are my fingers hurtin' you right now?"

"No," she said closing her eyes because the stimulating things I was doing to her body had her on chill.

"If you can let go like that while I'm inside you, I promise it won't hurt. Even if it does it won't hurt for long. I promise you it'll feel good." My lips were on her back and I had added another finger.

"Mmm," she moaned as I used my other hand to stimulate her clit.

Just when she started to get into it, I lifted her fine ass up and sat her on top of the counter.

"Open that pussy up for daddy," I instructed before proceeding to finger that sweet, fat muthafucka. "Damn, she is sooooo pretty."

Her muscles contracted and then released so that I could penetrate her deeper with my fingers. "You feel that ma?" I asked.

"Yesssss...." She wiggled her body showing that what she was feeling was pleasurable. I could also tell because her nipples and her clit were hard as hell.

I slid the condom off and put on another one. It was a good thing I had them on deck in almost every drawer in the crib. My player lifestyle came in handy even while I was in a relationship.

"Now, I want you to relax, okay Baby."

She nodded. "Okay."

I slid inside of her sloppy snatch and held on her to her chunky little ass cheeks. "Mmmm…"

Her muscles held me in place, but then I felt them relax so I could go a little deeper. "Just like that ma. You okay?"

"Uhhh…mmm hmmm, damn Zy," she moaned with her hand on my chest. "That's deep."

I moved it away. "No hands until after you take all this dick."

She bit her bottom lip and closed her eyes as I gently pushed my dick all the way inside. When I felt her wetness on my balls and there was no cool air on my shit, only the warmth of her insides, I knew I was in there. At first I didn't move. I just enjoyed feeling my entire length covered by her walls. Damn, her muscles were massaging my shit.

"You good ma? It hurt?" I looked down at her face to make sure that she was okay.

She nodded and looked up at me with vulnerable eyes. "I'm good baby." Her voice was a sexy whisper.

"Am I hurtin' you?"

"Not…really…"

I moved a little bit hoping that it would loosen her up some. It was a thin line between tight and too tight, but it was a good thing she got super wet.

"Ohhh…mmm…keep doin' that. That feels good. Mmm," she moaned and started to move her hips around for me.

"Yeah, there you go Baby…mmm…that's what I'm talkin' 'bout…" I leaned over and kissed her long and deep.

Shit, a nigga had fucked up now. If I thought I was gone before, I hadn't seen a damn thing yet.

Chapter 10

Beyanka

"That hoe was tryna act all cray, but as you can see, it's been a week and that bitch ain't showed up again. I told her this is where I'll be," I bragged with a Corona in one hand and a blunt that was almost gone in the other. It was burning my finger tips, so I dropped it in the ashtray before it ruined my nails.

Mackie shook her head. "I ain't had no issues out of Kia's ass either. I think that's only because I blocked her ass on Facebook and I wasn't following her on Instagram anyway. Plus she don't know about Zy's pent house."

"Hmm. I told Cane he should move, but it ain't none of my business what he do wit' those hoes. I'm 'bout to be out in a lil' bit." I looked around Cane's living room and shook my head.

That nigga was living high on a hog and I was taking full advantage. I knew that in a week and a half he had spent close to fifty stacks on a bitch. He'd never had it put down on him like I had done. All of the strippers in Atlanta combined couldn't do what I did to his ass. That nigga had been whipped in no time, but it was time for me to go. I'd done all of the damage I could to Cane. It was time to move on, but until I left I was going to have a little bit more fun with him.

"What the hell is Cane and Zy doing down there. I'm ready to go eat. That nigga's tripping." Mackie sucked her teeth and started bouncing her leg impatiently.

"You prego or something? That's like the fifth time you said you're hungry since you been here. Zy told you that he had to handle some business," I said with a shrug of my shoulders.

I didn't think Mackie was really cut out for being a king pin's wifee. She and Zy loved each other, but she seemed to not understand the streets and the fact that the man was like a CEO. He owned and operated a major corporation that could rival any Fortune 500 company as far as profits and structure. Damn, my poor friend was so damn green.

"I'm not pregnant. I know he said he had to handle some business, but damn. We're supposed to already be sitting down at Benihana grubbing by now. Nah, he had to stop here first to handle some business," Mackie complained.

Cane walked up the steps that led to the fully furnished basement and made his way over to me.

"You wanna hit the blunt sexy?" He asked as he passed it to me.

I took it and took a pull. "You wanna hit it Mackie."

"Hell nah." She frowned and fanned the smoke out of her face. "I'm already hungry, so why the hell would I smoke that shit."

"Damn lil' ma. I'm sorry. Zy told me to tell you he'll be up here in a minute," Cane said. "Those three niggas ya'll seen come in are some young recruits. We tryna train 'em and shit, but sometimes the amateur can come out. One of them niggas was supposed to shoot this cat who tried to rob him on the block, but he missed after emptyin' a full clip. That nigga Zy's chewin' his ass the fuck out." Cane laughed as I passed him the blunt back.

"Which one is it?" I asked remembering one in particular because when he first came in he had touched my ass.

I gave that nigga a look, but decided not to start no shit. Even after Cane made it clear that we were fucking that nigga had the nerve to grab my ass even harder a second time. That time I grabbed his hand and told him that shit would cost him. I didn't specify whether that cost would be his life or some cash. Now that I knew he was probably a bitch ass nigga, I wanted to get him in even more shit. He'd learn not to touch a lady's ass for free.

"The one who had on the black and white A fitted with the cornrows," Cane said right before taking a tote of the blunt.

That was that nigga. "Word? That nigga touched my ass twice."

Cane gave me a look and put the blunt in the ash tray.

"Come look and make sure he's the right one," he said as he walked toward the steps.

Mackie got up too. "Let me tell this nigga to come on. Damn."

She followed us to the basement. When we walked in Zy was all up in that nigga's face. Just like I thought, the one Cane had described was the bitch ass nigga who kept copping feels on my ass and shit.

"You can't afford to be lettin' niggas take yo' shit and you waste fuckin' bullets on they ass! You losin' too much money mufucka! How you gon' be a Cue who can't fuckin' shoot…" When Zy heard the door close he looked up and his expression was one of anger.

"What the fuck Cane? Why the hell you bring them down here nigga? I'm comin' Baby, go upstairs," Zy hissed with his eyes still glued to Cane.

"Hold up patna. Is he the nigga?" Cane asked me as he pointed at the short, brown skinned dude who had felt me up.

He looked like he was about our age, but he was a loser in my eyes. That nigga didn't deserve to be a Cue. I was a boss bitch and I could pick a weak ass nigga out of a line up. That nigga was as weak as they come.

"Yup and he'll be the death of the Cues if ya'll fuck wit' him." I stuck my nose up in the air and whipped my '18 inch weave over my shoulder.

Cane nodded and just like that he pulled his 9 millimeter from the waist of his jeans. With one shot that nigga who touched my ass had a bullet hole in his left hand. The bullet went straight through and then got stuck in the wall.

"Fuck nigga!" Dude yelped and jumped up from his seat. "Owwww....damn...arggghhhhh!" That nigga grabbed his bleeding hand and fell to his knees in agonizing pain.

"What the hell Cane?" Zy asked not knowing what the hell was going on.

"Touch another ass in my fuckin' crib without my permission mufucka! That's my mufuckin' ass nigga! Learn how to bust yo' gun bitch ass nigga! Yo' hoe ass worried about puttin' your hands on some ass I'm fuckin'. That's my shit nigga! Don't touch my shit nigga!" Cane was going off and that shit turned me the fuck on.

Zy shook his head and nodded at the two other recruits. "Get that nigga outta here."

They grabbed the dude that Cane had shot and carried him up the steps. He was still screaming and crying. It sounded like he was a little boy instead of a grown man. I shook my head at how fucking lame he was.

Mackie just stared at me and shook her head.

"What? I didn't know that he was gonna shoot that nigga."

"Go upstairs and wait for me Baby. I need to talk to Cane. Do you mind goin' wit' her Bey?" Zy's eyes were stern and it was the first time I could see the malice in them. Seeing the love he felt for Mackie had made me underestimate him.

I nodded and led the way up the steps. Once we were in the living room Mackie went in on me.

"What the fuck is wrong with you?" She shook her head at me and all I could think about was how judgmental she could be at times.

"Ain't shit wrong wit' me Miss Perfect. What's wrong wit' you? Yo' mama used to sale weed and fuck a drug dealer bitch! Now you're in love wit' a fuckin' gangsta. Don't fuckin' judge me like you're better than me. Like I said, I had no way of knowin' that was gonna happen!" I rolled my eyes and tried my best not to slap her ass.

"This ain't about my mama, my daddy or me! This is about the fact that you enjoyed that shit! I could see it in your eyes Bey. It made you feel good that Cane was mad enough to shoot that nigga even if he didn't kill him. It probably turned your crazy ass on. Calling somebody else cray. Something is clearly wrong with you and I don't know how I didn't see it until now." She shook her head at me and walked toward the door. "Tell Zy I'll be in the car."

"Zy, Zy, Zy. Damn, all you can see is Zy's dick right now." That stopped her dead in her tracks and she turned around to face me.

"What the fuck did you say?" Mackie asked with her eyes glued to mine. She was mad and I could tell.

"I said all you can see is Zy's dick right now bitch! You fuckin' heard me! Dumb ass…"

Before I could even finish she was all up in my face. "Fuck you Bey! You're just jealous that I got a real relationship and as always you just fuckin' a nigga for some weave, or some fuckin' gel tips! If you gon' fuck, fuck for a come up bitch!"

I couldn't believe that hoe and just before I could punch her in the face Cane and Zy were up the steps breaking us up.

"Whoa, whoa, what the hell's goin' on?" Zy asked as he grabbed Mackie and pulled her away from me.

"What's up shawty?" Cane asked all up in my face as he held me against the wall. "What the hell? Ya'll girls. What you doin' yo'?"

"Fuck her!" I was so mad and I had never been that mad at Mackie before.

That bitch had crossed the fucking line. When I fucked a nigga I got way more than a weave and some damn gel tips. That bitch had me fucked up. Don't insult me like that hoe. Fucking friend or not.

"Can we just go please," she said to Zy.

"I'll holla at you later Cane," Zy said with his arm around her as they left.

Cane just looked at me like he knew that shit was all my fault.

"What the fuck just happened?"

I shrugged my shoulders. "She went off 'cause you shot dude like it was my fault. She claimed that I enjoyed that shit."

Cane wrapped his arms around me and started kissing on my neck.

"Mmm, damn…"

"Did you?"

"Did I what?" I knew what he meant.

"Did you enjoy that shit?"

His fingers were inside my panties, searching, reaching.

"Mmm…yessss." Damn, that shit felt good.

I did feel bad about what happened with Mackie, but I was glad that Cane was willing to get my mind off of it. He unbuttoned my shorts and I stepped out of them. My panties came off next.

"Turn around," he demanded.

"Put on a condom," I said with my eyes on him.

He rolled his eyes as he reached into his pocket for one. After he slid it on, I turned around and let him slide inside.

"Fuck me hard!" I tooted my ass up and opened my legs wider for him to go deeper.

Damn and he did.

*   *   *

Me and Cane were supposed to go out that night with Zy and Mackie, but after our argument I wasn't really up for going anywhere. The effects of the weed and alcohol had worn off and suddenly I was aware of what I'd said to my best friend. I was honestly just jealous of her and Zy's relationship just like she'd thrown in my face.

During the time I'd been there we'd all gone to Six Flags, The Underground, every strip club, almost every night club and every other hot spot in between. It was like I was forced to sit there and watch true love manifest in front of my eyes and all I ever seemed to have was a sex thing.

"You okay?" Cane asked with his head resting on my breasts.

We were watching an episode of Martin and I knew for a fact that I was unusually quiet. Shit, not only that, but I wasn't even in the mood for sex. The past couple hours were the longest we'd gone without doing anything sexual since the first night I was at his crib. When I looked around I wondered why the hell I was even there. My whole point of being in Atlanta was to visit my best friend, not trick off with some nigga.

"Not really. I'll be leavin' in a couple days and my best friend is mad at me." There was a pout on my face and for the first time in a while I actually had a conscience.

Cane kissed my cheek. "She won't stay mad baby. I'm sure this ain't ya'll first fight."

Did he just call me baby? "It ain't our first fight, but it's the first time we've almost gone to blows. I'm just glad ya'll stopped us, because then I'd really feel fucked up."

"You sure you don't wanna go out somewhere? It's still early."

For some reason I felt like he was really starting to care about me. Where had that come from in such a short amount of time? The rude, obnoxious dude I had met had been substituted with someone who seemed to be a lot more considerate.

"I am a little hungry. Let's go to Waffle House. I want some bacon, hash browns and waffles."

He nodded. "C'mon, 'cause I got the munchies like a mufucka."

On our way to his Audi truck he put his arm around my waist and kissed the top of my head.

"You remind me of an onion," Cane said.

"Huh?" I asked and shook my head. That man could say the craziest shit. Was he referring to my ass? Was that supposed to be a compliment? If so, it was lame as fuck. I had to laugh. "Are you tryna say I stink or somethin' nigga?"

He laughed too. "Nah shawty. Let me explain what I mean. When you cut into an onion at first it can be harsh and even make you cry. After that you realize that mufucka got a lot of layers and once you get used to it the tears go away. I think you come off a certain way, but it's really more to you than that. Shit, onions are so damn good that people cut them open anyway knowin' they goin' make their eyes burn. Some shit's just worth goin' through to get to the good part. So, you my onion and shit."

I let what he said sink in and it actually made good sense.

"Hmm, so I guess you my onion too." I even had a smile on my face when he opened the door and waited for me to climb in.

When he got behind the wheel I had to fuck with him.

"Wow. Who the hell is this gentleman? I never would've thought you had that shit in you. Let me find out you gon' miss me when I leave."

He drove off and glanced over at me. "I am gon' miss you. Straight up. It ain't like I ain't been enjoyin' your company and shit."

Damn, I had been enjoying him too, but I was still feeling a twinge a guilt about what had happened with Mackie. I even felt bad for what had happened to dude. That nigga had got shot in the hand over me and I didn't even know his name. It was crazy because I could've checked him myself for touching my ass, but for some reason I was starving for some drama. Maybe I was just starving for some attention. Having Cane show some kind of jealousy over me made me feel wanted.

"I been enjoyin' you too Cane, but I wish I was wit' my bestie right now." I sighed when I thought about how fucked up I must've made her feel.

Of course she wasn't going to agree with what I did or said. She never did. That was why we were so close. We balanced each other out, so that shit worked as crazy as our friendship seemed.

"Hmm, you two seem so different. How did ya'll become friends anyway?"

"We met in the third grade, but she went to a different school our fourth grade year. When we were in the fifth grade she came back and we've been close ever since." I kept the explanation vague because I felt like he really didn't care and it was just for the sake of conversation.

"Don't worry 'bout it. I'll get Zy to talk to her and we'll figure out how to get you two together so ya'll can work things out. Okay?" He stopped at a red light and turned to look at me. For a minute I thought I saw something real in his eyes.

Then he leaned over and kissed me, tongue and all. After all of that butt naked, freaky ass sex we'd been having and we were now sharing our first kiss. How backwards was that shit?

It was such an intense moment that neither one of us noticed the black van that stopped beside us on his side. When we finally broke our kiss I looked and saw the door of the van slide open. There were three men dressed in all black in ski masks. They were pointing the biggest guns I'd ever seen and I was stuck.

Cane looked back and when he saw them he yelled, "Get down!"

I suddenly snapped out of it and managed to squeeze my body down on the floor between the dashboard and my seat. Cane put his body over mine to shield me, which surprised me in the mist of such a crazy moment. The sound of shattering glass and gun fire made me cover my ears as I sobbed.

POW! POW! POW! POW! POW!

TAT! TAT! TAT! TAT! TAT!

Chapter 11

Zyon

"Damn, that nigga still ain't answerin'," I said shaking my head.

I was trying to call Cane because he knew that he was supposed to be handling some business for me while I dealt with the shit with Duke. He'd shot me a text a couple hours before saying that he was on it, but he hadn't done shit. Nobody had even seen his ass. Now that nigga was ignoring my calls and shit. That was the shit that I was talking about right there. When it came to getting some ass that was all that nigga was focused on.

Mackie glanced over at me. "I hope everything's okay. Maybe I should try calling Bey"

"Yeah, I know ya'll pissed at each other, but see if she'll answer," I agreed.

She made the call and put the phone on speaker. Bey's phone went straight to voicemail.

"You think something happened?" She asked with a worried look on her face.

"Nah. They probably just fuckin' and shit." I shook my head. "That nigga."

Baby had been fucked up about her argument with old girl, so I gave her a hug and rested my chin on top of her head.

"I feel so bad. Bey's always been like that and I've been her friend all this time. For some reason the people who are close to me tend to be so different from me, but I wonder if I'm really so different. I think I've been close to Bey for so long because she does all the things that I want to do, but can't. She's like my sister and no matter what she said I shouldn't have let it get to that point. I'm supposed to be the level headed one, but am I really?"

It was obvious that she was crying, but she wasn't boo hooing or nothing. I rubbed her back and kissed the top of her head.

"You and your girl'll work it out ma. Friends fight all the time. The two of you may have said some things you didn't mean, but if your friendship is solid you'll be able to move on from this. Don't worry," I said soothingly.

"I just got a bad feeling that something's happened. What if that bitch Ne Ne went over there and started some shit. Anything could've happened."

"I'll stop by Cane's spot. It's on the way to my pops crib and I gotta scoop him. You gon' be okay while I'm gone?" I pulled away to take a look at her face.

Her eyes were all red and swollen because she hadn't stopped crying since her argument with Bey. We decided to order the food from Benihana, but we didn't eat in. Instead we went back to my crib, because everything that was going on was taking a toll on her.

"I don't know Zy. I want to say that I will, but I honestly don't know." She kissed the side of my mouth and then my lips. "But I know that you have to take care of that shit with Duke, so I won't bitch."

I sighed and stood up. Reaching out to take her hand, I pulled her up from the sofa and wrapped my arms around her waist. She reached up and wrapped her arms around my neck. When I squeezed she squeezed even tighter.

"I love you woman."

"I love you too man."

We shared a laugh.

I loosened our embrace to look at her, but I didn't let her go. "I am promisin' you right now that I will be comin' back home to you tonight. I love you too much to let something happen to me ma. You hear me?"

"Loud and clear baby."

I could tell that she was fighting back tears and I felt like shit. Damn, she made me question all of the shit that I thought was important before I met her. True, the Cues were like my family, but she had become my family. With her I could have a family. If I kept putting my life in jeopardy would I even have that chance? Yet and still, I had a strong attraction to the streets and the lifestyle that I lived. I loved that shit, but I loved Baby even more.

Then I thought about Caruso. Pops told me that he had some family connections in Brooklyn who were digging for information on his whereabouts. At that point they had nothing and I didn't even know where to start. Shit, I hadn't been to New York in years and my Auntie didn't even want to talk about Caruso.

When I stared down at my woman, I wondered if I should put her in the position to worry about me over and over again. The situation with Caruso would really have her stressed out. Maybe it would be best to postpone my trip up top until after she started school. Then she would be preoccupied with something else to put her energy in.

I kissed the tip of her pretty little nose and then her sexy lips. "I gotta go."

She nodded while our lips were still joined and whispered, "Okay."

When she closed her eyes the tears she'd been holding back slid down her cheeks and made my heart stir. I wiped them away and kissed her again; deeper than before. Without looking at her again, because I wouldn't have left if I did, I made my way to the door. There was no way I could see her cry and still go out to do what I knew could take me away from her. It hurt me like hell to leave my lady in tears.

*   *   *

I had been knocking on Cane's door for a good minute before I finally decided to leave. When I got in the car I called Baby.

"Hello." Her voice sounded stronger than it had when I left her, so that made me feel a little bit better.

"Hey ma."

"Sup babe?"

"I'm good. You good?"

"I'm good." I could hear a smile in her voice.

"Well, I stopped at Cane's and his Audi ain't here. I rung the doorbell and knocked on the door, but ain't nobody answer. I figured Bey is either knocked out or wit' him wherever he is. That nigga gon' catch it. Now I'm gon' have to get somebody else to handle that shit for me. I'm on the way to Pop's spot. I just wanted to let you know what's goin' on."

"Okay babe, thank you. You were right. Those freaks are probably at a strip club some damn where," she said.

I drove off. "Yup. So, what you doin' ma?"

I was trying my best to get her mind off what she was stressing about even if I wasn't there.

"Writing."

I knew that she liked to write poetry, so it wasn't anything new for her to use that art form as an outlet.

"What you writin' beautiful?"

"A poem for you."

"For me? Really?" I couldn't help but smile. "You gon' read it to me."

"I'm going to read it to you, but not right now. It's not done yet." Her voice sounded so sweet.

"Okay my love. Look, my Pops is callin', so I'm gonna call you back."

She sighed. "K babe. Love you."

"Love you more." I clicked over.

"I'm on my way Pops."

"A'ight," he said.

We talked for a few minutes and then I tried to call Cane again. The phone just rang, so I hung up and called Duke.

"Wassup Zy?"

"Not much my nigga. I was just checkin' to see if you was at the spot."

"Nah nigga. I just got back yesterday, so I'm out makin' some plays."

"Hmm. When we talked earlier you said you'd meet me at the spot 'round ten."

"Ah shit. Right, right. I'm sorry dude, but it's gon' have to be later tonight."

"How much later and what kinda plays man? I mean, we both know what time it is. I say we need to meet, we need to meet."

"Look man. I got some shit I gotta take care of, but I feel ya. How 'bout you meet me somewhere. I just won't be close to Candler."

Damn, that nigga acted like he was calling the fucking shots.

"If this shit wasn't as pressin' as it is I'd say fuck it, but this shit gotta be done. Where you gon' be nigga?"

He gave me the address and I plugged it into my GPS.

"A'ight. I'll be there in 'bout forty five."

*   *   *

"I want to fuck Caruso up for what he did to my mama, but I love Mackie and I hate to keep stressin' her out," I explained to Diablo.

"I feel ya Zy. For real. I love Yanna and I always have. When I used to cheat wit' hoes, or do street shit it would fuck wit' me so hard. Shit, I could only imagine what it did to her. I knew that I could kill a nigga quick, or serve a fiend wit' no problem, but hurtin' her always fucked wit' me. That's how you know you love Mackie. It be plenty of hoes you don't mind hurtin', but when you find the right chick it kills you to hurt her. She's the one young buck," he said with a serious ass look on his face.

"You think so?" I asked although I knew that shit all along. Having the approval of my Pops meant the world to me although I would never admit it.

Shit, it wasn't like I could get my mother's approval.

"Think? I know nigga. I know how I felt the moment I fell in love wit' Yanna. It became a time when she was the only thing on my mind. I didn't give a fuck about my money or none of that shit. It was all about her. Even when I was fuckin' other hoes, it was all about her. I gotta give it to you Young Buck. You sho' got more self control than I did."

I laughed. "That's 'cause I lost my mom. Women are like a commodity to me."

"I lost my mom too, but for some reason I still took women for granted. That was probably because I had Merlia and Aunt Mona," he said before looking up at me with a regretful look on his face.

I nodded. "I can't wait to meet Aunt Mona and Aunt Merlia is an angel."

"She and Unc will be here in a few months and you're right about that."

"What you think gon' go down?" I asked him. He was the veteran and he'd once held my title.

"I don't know Zy. I got yo' back young buck. That's all I know."

*   *   *

"Your destination is on the right," the feminine voice of the GPS stated in a British accent.

When I looked I noticed that we were pulling up to what looked like an abandoned warehouse. I had no clue why Duke would ask us to meet him there. Something told me that it was a set up and that nigga already knew that I had killed his cousin Ro.

"I got a feelin' that something ain't right," Diablo said with his eyes peeled on our surroundings. "You ready to kill that nigga if you got too?"

"Hell fuckin' yeah," I said vehemently.

"A'ight. You see that nigga's car?"

I looked around. "Yeah," I said as I pointed.

"Ah shit," my pops said at the same time that I noticed two police cruisers parked too. "This shit might just be a set up. Fuck, let's get the hell outta here. Yanna'll kill me if I get locked up tonight."

I was just about to press the gas when I saw two police officers walking toward one of the cruisers with Duke and that nigga Cam in handcuffs.

"What the fuck?" I asked nobody in particular.

"Nigga, get the hell outta here before them mufuckas come ask us what the fuck we doin' here." I could tell by the look on Diablo' s face that he wasn't trying to be caught up in no bullshit.

"A'ight." I nodded and discreetly turned into the parking lot of the building next to our destination.

Before getting back on the road, I hit the lights and waited for the cops to pass by. I couldn't help but wonder what the hell had just happened. What the hell had Duke and Cam been hemmed up for?

"Shit," I said under my breath as I wondered what the hell was going to happen next.

"The only thing about seein' yo' niggas get knocked is not knowin' if they gon' roll on you or not," Pops said thoughtfully. "Everybody claims to be loyal, but they don't always show it."

Hmm. That was some real shit. I knew for a fact that loyalty was a rare thing in the hood. When it came to getting less time, some niggas didn't give a fuck about being a rat. The no snitch rule was often disobeyed when it came down to a nigga getting some real prison time.

"You sho' right about that man."

My phone rang and I reached in my pocket while I steered with the other hand. I didn't even bother to look at the screen before answering, because traffic was thick and I needed my eyes on the road.

"Yo'."

"Zy, wassup nig, it's Cane man."

"Cane? What the fuck man? I been tryna call you..."

"Nigga, some mufuckas pulled up beside me and Bey and started blastin' and shit. If them niggas had shot up the body of the truck too we'd both be dead as hell. Good thing they only shot through the windows. Guess them niggas was tryna get a head shot. I got hit in the shoulder and had to get some fragments removed from my shit from the blasts. It was only bits and pieces though. No major shit. A nigga been drugged up," he explained quickly.

"Shit, how's Bey man. Mackie's gon' flip out if something happened to her girl." I shook my head as I thought about that shit.

"She's right here my nigga. Make sure you let Mackie know what's goin' on a'ight. Her girl's goin' through it and she left her phone at the crib. When those niggas pulled off the cops came quick as hell and from there they called the ambulance. First mufuckas I saw when I woke up was detectives askin' me a million fuckin' questions. I'on know who did that shit, but when I find out. Shit, a mufucka gon' pay!"

"Hmm, well nigga, I'm glad you and Bey good. I'm 'bout to head to the crib and let Baby know what's goin' on."

"Oh yeah. What happened wit' that nigga Duke?"

I quickly filled him in on Duke and Cam's arrest.

"What, you know what they got 'em for?"

"Nah, but I'm 'bout to make some calls and see what's up? What hospital you at my nig?"

"Dekalb Medical. I'm gettin' out of here tonight. I'on care what they say about me needin' to stay at least 'till tomorrow. Kiss my ass. I gotta find out who bucked at me, so I can end them mufuckas."

"I feel you man. Hit me when you leave. A'ight?"

"Bet that my nigga."

When he hung up my Pops went into interrogation mode.

"What was that all about?"

I filled him in on Cane's Audi getting shot up while he and Bey were inside.

"Damn, same ol' shit, just a different day."

"Hmm, you can say that shit again," I agreed.

*   *   *

Mackie

When the door opened and Zy stepped inside, I felt so damn relieved. I had worried every single second that he was gone, but I put on a strong front for him. Instead of jumping into his arms like I wanted to, I decided to play it calm. I didn't want him to think that I couldn't handle what came with his lifestyle.

"Hey Baby," he said as he walked over to sit beside me on the sofa.

There was a smile on his face, but I could tell that something was wrong. It wasn't his usual cocky smile. Nope. The smile that he was wearing looked more like he was nervous about something.

"Sup babe." I smiled before he planted a soft, wet kiss on my lips.

"Uh, I talked to Cane," he said before letting me know about what had happened.

"Oh my God! If she had been shot I would've felt horrible. Thank goodness they're both okay."

He rubbed my shoulders and tried to soothe me with his words. "I'm sure you two will see each other tomorrow and your friendship will be back to normal."

"I sure hope so, but what happened with you and Duke tonight?"

"Shhhh." Zy shook his head. "We not gon' talk about Duke right now."

I gave him a look that let him know that there would be nothing else going on other than him letting me know what the hell had happened.

"Don't do that Zy."

"What?" He asked innocently.

"Don't shut me out and not let me know what the fuck is going on. I don't care if you think that what you do out there will bother me. I need to know the truth and I need to get used to it. I know that you want to keep what we have and the streets separate, but truthfully, I need to know certain shit whether you want me to or not."

"You're right ma, but I don't want to talk about that shit right now. I just wanna chill wit' you and forget about what goes on out there." He pointed toward the window in reference to the streets. "You're my escape Baby and when I'm wit' you I don't even wanna think about that shit. So, I feel you, but it's a time and a place for everything and this ain't it. I'll tell you all about it tomorrow. Okay?"

He cupped my chin in his hand and tongued me down like only his fine ass could. Damn, he'd shut me up once again.

"Okay," I agreed knowing that the happy moment we were about to share would be far and few between. It was best to enjoy it.

As he pulled out a sack of weed and a Swisher, I thought of my best friend almost getting killed and the possibility of him and Duke going to war. It had me all fucked up. Still, I smiled like nothing was bothering me in the world. Truthfully, the thought of me being in danger while I was with Zy had crossed my mind over and over again. Was my mother right? Was I safe with him?

*   *   *

"Girl, that nigga actually covered me and shit. I was so fuckin' shocked. That shit just proved to me that he's not the dude I thought he was. I mean, he really seems to care and shit," Beyanka said as she stuffed her mouth with a slice of pizza.

We'd decided to go to Little Five Points Pizza, which was one of me and Zy's favorite spots. Little Five Points or Little Five as some called it, was a commercial district not far from downtown Atlanta. There were all kinds of places to shop, restaurants, tattoo parlors and a cultural melting pot of people. Some would describe it as where the "artsy" or "bohemian" crowd came out to shop, eat and have fun.

"I'm just glad that you're okay," I said.

We'd already apologized, hugged and made up. Shit, she could've been killed, so I wasn't going to waste any more time being mad at my best friend.

"Me too girl, but I feel so bad for not bein' there when you talked to your mom. When I went to get my stuff a few days ago, she was actin' really nonchalant about what's goin' on, but I can tell that she feels horrible. Have you talked to her?"

I threw my crust down on my plate and took a swig of my iced tea.

"No and I don't want to right now. It's not fair that she automatically cut me off for not doing what she wants me to do. She always told me not to let a man control me, but it's okay if she does. Whether she knows it or not, she's the one who tries to control me. I'm sick of it, so I'll show her that I can take care of myself. I love my mama, but I love Zy too. She made me choose, so it is what is."

Bey sighed and wiped her mouth with a napkin. She drained her lemonade and then belched.

"Eww, rude ass bitch," I joked.

She laughed. "Excuse me, but anyways, I feel where you're comin' from. You only get one mama though. One of you have to try to get through to the other."

"Hmm. Won't be me," I hissed dismissing my bestie's attempt to convince me to make up with my mother.

"You're so damn stubborn." She shook her head at me.

"Me? Stubborn? Bitch please. Your ass is the one that's stubborn."

"Whatever. We had a disagreement and we're talkin' right now."

"Totally different situation Bey."

She narrowed her eyes at me. "The same way you felt the need for us to kiss and make up is the same way you should feel about you and your mom kissing and making up. If something happens to her you'll regret not talkin' to her and you know it."

I sighed and sat back in my seat. "Damn, I'm full."

Bey shook her head at me. "You just gon' act like I ain't say what I said huh?"

"Nope. I'm just not going to respond to it. You done?"

Bey looked at the two slices of cheese pizza that we had left. "Yeah, I'm full too. I'll go get a box."

I wasn't asking if she was done with the pizza. I was asking if she was done trying to convince me to do something I wasn't going to do. She got up to go get a takeout box and I just sat there and thought about what she'd said. I wanted to make things right with my mother, but I hadn't done anything wrong. I felt that she should be the one to reach out to me, since she was the one who'd started everything.

Bey came back to our booth and put the pizza in the box.

"You ready?" She asked. "I gotta get back and take care of Cane."

"Yeah, but let me find out that you feelin' that nigga."

She just smiled as I got up and followed her out of the restaurant. My mind was still telling me that I had no reason to apologize to my mom.

*   *   *

When I walked in the crib I heard Zy talking to somebody on the phone. As I made my way over to him, he flashed me a smile. I leaned over to kiss him and sat down to wait for him to end his call.

"A'ight man. I'll hit you up later." He hung up and got up from his favorite leather recliner to join me.

"Everything good babe?" I asked as I kissed him again. Damn, I loved that man so much.

"Mmm hmm." He kept right on kissing me, but I wanted to talk.

He still hadn't told me anything about Duke and I wanted to know what had happened or what was going to happen. When he finally pulled away, I started with the questions.

"So, is this finally the time and place for us to talk about what happened last night with Duke?"

He let out a sigh and then looked away. I hated when he did that shit, so I cleared my throat to get his attention back on the subject at hand.

"Hello. I asked you a question."

He looked at me. "And I heard you ma. Look, I talked to my pops about that today. He told me that it's best for me to be real and straight up wit' you about what goes on just like I would be if I had any other job. He said that's how he and Yanna made it all these years. So, I'm not gonna sugar coat shit. I need you to be prepared for anything. Last night we went to meet up wit' Duke, but when we got to the spot the cops had him and Cam in handcuffs and shit. Before then my niggas had told me about these two cats who kept poppin' up on Glenwood who claimed they were from Macon. Those niggas had been on the block askin' for work and Duke and Cam took the bait. The spot we pulled up to was where the deal was supposed to go down at. Them niggas who claimed that they were from Macon were the Feds the whole time. I knew that it was either that or they were jack boys. It's fucked up 'cause them niggas were doin' plays behind my back and shit. I guess he thought his lil' business venture would be done by the time I got there. Shit's crazy 'cause I still don't know if he knows about me killin' his cousin and shit. Then that nigga Cam was probably feelin' that bitch Kia more than he wanna admit. I'm just gon' sit and wait to see if them niggas gon' run they mouth or not. No worries though babe. I keep my hands clean and I got my lawyer on deck. I'm gon' give you his info though, just in case shit go left and shit."

Damn, that shit was cray cray. Now my man had to worry about whether he would be given up for a plea deal. It was no telling what them niggas got caught with and conspiracy carried way more time than actually selling some shit.

"Wow," I breathed as I shook my head. "What now babe?"

He shrugged his shoulders. "Only time will tell. We just gotta be ready Baby."

I sighed and rested my head on his chest. "Nothing's gonna take you away from me."

He rubbed my back as he held me tightly in his arms. No matter what my mother had said, I felt safe in them.

*   *   *

"What the fuck do you mean the condom came off nigga!"

Zy had a look on his face that made me think that he'd known that the condom was off, but just didn't bother to tell me. If I found out that nigga had took it off on purpose, I was going to kick his ass.

"Look babe, your pussy's tight as hell and your muscles must've pulled it off when I was pullin' out. I promise you it was on the whole time."

I was laying there with my legs wide open as he pushed his finger inside of me to find the lost condom.

"Shit, what if some of your sperm is inside me? I can't get pregnant right now Zy," I whined with tears in my eyes.

He sucked his teeth at me in annoyance. "If you get pregnant it won't be the end of the world."

"Not only do I have to worry about getting pregnant, but what about the bitches you fucked before me like Kia?"

"I never fucked Kia raw and any chick before her I wrapped up wit'. Shit, I always wrap up wit' you, but shit happens shorty. Damn. Look, if it makes you feel better we can both go to the clinic and get tested for everything. Then you can get some birth control pills just in case this happens again."

"That is if I ain't already knocked up!" I snapped.

"Relax baby. I can feel the condom okay, but you gotta relax so I can pull it out," he said being calm despite the fact that I was being a real bitch about the shit.

I took a deep breath and tried to relax my muscles. It was a good thing I was wet, because that nigga was digging up in my shit like I was having a pap smear.

"I got it," he said as he finally got a grip on it. "Your pussy's so damn wet and shit that it was hard as hell to get that mufucka."

He got up to flush it and I got up to douche and then take a shower. It was a good thing I'd gone on a toiletry run the day before.

Once we were in the bed, he pulled me close to him so we could spoon.

"You mad at me?" He asked.

"No, but I don't know why you didn't know that the condom was off until you pulled out. I just hope you're not lying to me. I hope if you would've felt the difference you would've told me," I said.

He kissed my neck. "I'm tellin' you the truth babe. It didn't come off until I pulled out. Your shit was squeezin' all tight like it didn't wanna let go and that's why the condom came off. You ain't pregnant ma, but if by some miracle you are, we gon' handle that. I won't turn my back on you. I promise."

I knew that he wouldn't, but I wasn't ready for motherhood. My life had always been structured and in order. There was no way a baby was in my plans right now. I would be going to Spellman soon to finish up my Business degree. Children would have to come later and that would be after at least a year or two of marriage.

"Okay Zy," I said not really feeling the whole damn situation. Shit, I was frustrated as hell and I didn't feel like talking about it anymore.

"Night babe. Love you."

"Love you too."

I was so glad he'd gotten the hint, but it was hard as hell for me to fall asleep.

Chapter 12

Zyon

"Caruso's been MIA for two years. Nobody knows where he is, or so they claim. He's wanted by the FBI and right before they could bring him in he just vanished. At the time he was married to a woman named Maria Livingston who lives in Staten Island now, but of course she says she has no idea where he is either. The man's somewhere out there, but even the Feds can't find him," my pops explained to me as we sipped coffee at the Pancake House on Cheshire Bridge Road.

I shook my head in disbelief. "Shit, so what now? How we gon' find that mufucka?"

"I got somebody on it and believe me, that muthafucka can be found. It just may take a little bit longer than we expected."

"Damn," I said under my breath.

Almost two weeks had passed and I was ready to move along with my revenge plot on Caruso. It seemed that it wasn't going to go down anytime soon and I was mad as fuck. The thing was, I thought I'd finally be able to get it over with. After all of those years of being distracted by other shit, I finally felt that it was time to get rid of that muthafucka once and for all. My mother was my life and I'd do anything to feel that she was finally resting in peace.

"Don't even sweat it young buck. We gon' get him. A'ight?" My pops gave me a reassuring look.

I nodded. "Enough about that mufucka. How's Yanna and the baby?"

"Good man. Good. I like it when she's pregnant. It brings out her sensitive side."

I smiled at that. "What my lil' bro been up to?"

Diablo smiled all big at the mention of his youngest son Peanut. "Video games and sports man. That's all that lil' nigga talk about. He won't put that basketball you gave him down. He walks around the house wit' it all day and shit when he ain't pracin' his jump shot."

I chuckled. "That's my lil' man. I gotta call him today. He asked me to get some game for him, but I'm sure Yanna won't approve."

Shit, I wanted my younger brother to be different from me and our pops. Diablo agreed. We'd talked several times about how to keep him away from that life, but still make him into a man who could defend himself and the ones he loved.

"You know how she is, but she means well. One thing about her is that she didn't want kids at first, because she wanted them to have a different life than us. It's a catch 22 though. If we shelter him, the shit that happened to his Uncle Lamar could happen to him." He sighed.

Damn, that was some deep shit. My father had saved his own sister's life when he was ten. Some men had broken into their house and shot his parents. He took it upon himself to grab his father's gun from a drawer, load it and kill both of the men who killed his parents before they could kill him or Merlia. His father Cue had taught him how to shoot when he was as young as seven, so he wanted to teach Peanut how to defend himself too.

Unfortunately Merlia's husband Lamar was shot and killed a few months ago by someone who broke into their house to rob them. Ayanna was 'bout that life, so she shot the perpetrator before he could hurt Merlia or her children Cayleb and Caylee. Lamar and Merlia didn't believe in having a gun in the house, but I wonder if they did would things have turned out differently for him.

"I know what you mean Pops."

"I don't really want that shit for you either, but I already know that's who you are. If it was up to me, I would've been there to make sure you never became a Cue."

I could see the regret in his eyes.

"We'll just make sure that Peanut doesn't."

He nodded, but didn't say anything. Instead he looked out of the window to keep me from seeing the emotion on his face. That shit made me wonder what kind of man I would be at his age. Me and Mackie had gone to the clinic and found out that we were both clean. Her period came on the following week, so we figured she wasn't pregnant since it was normal. If she was pregnant I don't know how that would've affected me. I just made sure that I paid for her birth control pills and used condoms faithfully. Truth be told, I wasn't really ready for a baby either.

"Well shit. Let's get outta here," I said as I threw my napkin on my plate.

Pops cleared his throat and then looked at me with solemn eyes. "A'ight young buck."

*   *   *

My next stop after dropping my pops off was to the stash house to pick up my money. Deniro and Mel had been sure to stack and band up my cut for the week before I even got there. The rest of the money would be distributed accordingly. In other words it was pay day. I had the five million that we had got off of the Columbians in Miami in the safe at the crib, so I was stacking bread. A nigga loved to see my money pile up. It let me know that the life I had chosen was damn sure worth it. My plan was to pick up something nice for Baby before I headed to the crib. She was going to be moving out soon and I was going to miss her waiting for me when I came home.

"So, them niggas Duke and Cam was fuckin' doin' a side deal wit' them FED niggas who claimed to be from Macon wit' my dope? Muthafuckas," I spat angrily as I put the duffle bag full of money in my trunk.

"Yup, twenty keys of yo' shit. Sneaky ass niggas. His cousin Ro was up here 'cause he was doin' some side shit wit' him too," Deniro said with a blunt between his fingers like always.

"Hell yeah," Mel spoke up. "I'm fuckin' pissed off 'cause he and Cam knew that shit the whole time. Shit, they was the ones who told us about them niggas and shit to try and throw us off. The whole time they was on some shady shit. I swear. You can't trust niggas man, for real. I wonder if they gon' start runnin' their mouths. If them niggas ain't loyal in the streets they ain' t goin' be loyal behind that fuckin' cage."

"True true," I nodded in agreement. "For now we just gon' have to wait and see what's gon' happen. We gotta keep business boomin' 'cause we got that weight. It ain't no need to sit on it. If the cops start showin' up in the hood on that fuck shit we'll strategize our next move. In the meantime let's keep gettin' this money."

Deniro and Mel both slapped me fives because the feeling was mutual.

"Hell yeah my nigga. We just gon' be careful wit' how we make moves and shit," Mel said with a nod as Deniro passed him the blunt. "Word is that nigga knew that you killed his fam from the jump. His plan was to merk you after the deal and pretend them fuck niggas from Macon did it. Like we didn't know you wasn't involved in that shit."

"That mufucka talkin' about he was makin' a play. The whole time that nigga was playin' me. Merk me? Hmm. I got something for them niggas though. Get in touch wit' that nigga Mouse. He just waitin' to be sentenced and you know he'll merk them niggas quick. All he need is the word. The county ain't prison, but it's still easy to kill a nigga in that bitch. We gon' just have to shut him and Cam up before they can name anybody," I stated.

"If they ain't already," Mel said passing me the blunt. "Since he couldn't kill you givin' you to the FEDS is probably the next best thing. You know that nigga ain't got no bail."

I took a pull. "It won't really matter if they dead either way." As I blew the smoke out I thought about that nigga Mouse.

He had been locked up in the county for three months because of a double homicide that happened right in the drive through of the McDonald's on Candler Road. He had killed a King named T Dawg and his girlfriend as they ordered their food in broad daylight. That nigga didn't care.

Although we called him Mouse, he wasn't a small guy. He was about 6'3 and dark skinned with waist length locks. He was originally from Jamaica and he didn't take no shit. When the cops pulled him over after he jumped on 20 West to head back to the city he didn't even deny his guilt. As a matter of fact he told them that he'd kill those blood clots again if he could.

The reason behind the murder was the fact that T Dawg had tried to rob the trap that Mouse was working on Glenwood. That shit was bananas because when he ran up in the spot with a ski mask and a .45 Mouse took that nigga's gun away from his ass like it wasn't shit. That nigga P Dawg made a run for it to his car and Mouse had missed when he shot at him. Of course P. Dawg had some scared ass nigga driving the getaway car. He found out a few days later that P Dawg had been the culprit.

The next day Mouse followed that nigga from his girlfriend's apartment on Candler Road to the McDonald's and finished the job. At that point he didn't know who was driving the getaway car for P Dawg and he didn't care. He'd ended a beef that he'd wanted to end for a long time. He never liked that nigga P. Dawg and so he was really determined to merk that nigga.

"We on it," Deniro said. "I'm expectin' a call from that nigga Mouse today and shit. I'll let him know what to do in G code."

"Bet that. I'm 'bout to head on out though. Ya'll niggas hold it down a'ight," I said pounding them up before I got behind the wheel.

"Already," they said at the same time.

At least it was two niggas I could really trust other than my pops.

*   *   *

Mackie

I had woke up to another nightmare and reached over to feel for Zy, but he was gone. When I called him he said that he was having breakfast with his pops and then he had to make a few stops before he came home. I didn't bother to tell him about my nightmare because I didn't want him to worry. It was getting harder and harder for me to accept the past and I thought that time would make things easier.

After taking a long, hot bubble bath and smoking a half a blunt that Zy had left in the ashtray, I started to relax. Suddenly there was clarity and I felt like I knew what I needed to do. I opened my laptop and went to Facebook. I made a fake profile and used the name Kimberly Richardson. After that I went to Google and found a picture of a pretty brown skinned girl who looked like she who about thirteen. I saved it and used as a profile picture.

Once my page was set up I sent out about one hundred random friend requests. Of course I sent Roderick Lewis one and then I turned my computer off and went into the kitchen. I hoped his perverted ass would take the bait and wouldn't be suspicious because there was only one picture on the page. It was about time that I served him the payback that he deserved.

*   *   *

"Girl, I'm so excited about movin' down there!" Beyanka said sounding all hyped up.

After her near death experience with Cane she was claiming to be in love with him. By some divine miracle my best friend was talking about being exclusive to one man. I was surprised as hell. I was also a little skeptical about us being roommates, but neither of us wanted to move in with Zy or Cane too soon. It was only right that we got a place together.

She would be there in a week and after finding the perfect condo near Spellman's campus I was all set to move. One thing I wasn't looking forward to was possibly running into my mother when I went to get my things from Princess and Tre's. I was hoping that I could find a moment when she wasn't there to do it. She was also moving soon and I had no idea where. At that point it didn't even matter being that I wasn't welcome there anyway.

"I'm excited too. You're gonna love the place. It's so close to everything. You know Morehouse is close by. Eye candy all day." I laughed knowing damn well I wasn't even thinking about another man.

"It's okay to look, but I'm all into my Cane now."

"Are you really serious Bey? I mean, you know how you get into fazes when it comes to men. You're gonna move down here and everything. Wow."

She laughed. "I know you think I'm just goin' through the motions, but right before what happened me and that nigga had a moment. The fact that we both survived lets me know that we were meant to be. I gotta at least give it a try."

I sighed. "Okay, but I gotta warn you about him. He's a hoe."

"It don't matter now. I got that nigga all fucked up and I ain't worried about another bitch. Not even that hoe Ne Ne. He said he ain't seen her since that day she busted his Mercedes up."

"He ever find out who shot at ya'll? Zy ain't mentioned it."

"Nah, he told me that they were tryna find out, but ain't got nothin' so far."

Just then Zy walked through the door with a bouquet of red roses in his hand and a small rectangular box that was wrapped up in pretty baby blue paper and a white bow. He leaned over and kissed me. Damn, I felt dizzy when he pulled away.

"I'm gonna call you back Bey. My baby just got here."

"Tell Zy I said what's up."

"Bey said what's up baby?"

"Sup Bey!"

After ending the call I got up to grab the roses and put them on the mantle.

"They're gorgeous."

"You're gorgeous," he said just as I turned around to face him.

After he kissed me again he pulled away and gave me the box.

"This is for you my love."

I smiled up at him as I carefully tore the paper off. The black velvet box gave away the fact that it was a piece of jewelry. When I opened it and saw the beautiful gold charm bracelet I smiled.

"This is so pretty," I gasped as I passed it to him to put it on me.

There was only one charm on it and it was very meaningful. It was an incursive letter A and I already knew what it represented before he could even explain it.

"We're both from different states, but coming to the A is probably the best thing that ever happened to the both of us. We found love here and it's no tellin' what else life has in store. Ever so often I'm gonna add a charm to remind you of our life together. Maybe one day you can pass it on to our daughter and she can pass it on her daughter and so on."

When he looked up at me he had to see the tears glistening in my eyes. I softly touched his face.

"Damn, I love you."

"I know mami. I love you too."

"I know papi. Now let's make love in the A...in the A." I was singing to the tune of Love In This Club by Usher.

Zy smiled sexily at me as he unbuttoned my shorts and helped me get out of them. Then he dropped down to his knees and I knew what that meant. I closed my eyes and enjoyed the way his warm, wet tongue felt as it snaked up my inner thigh. That nigga wanted to tease me, but I knew that he would have his mouth full of pussy in no time.

*   *   *

As we lay in the bed all cuddled up together I told him all about my nightmare. He held on to me tightly as I cried and told him all about my plan for Roderick Lewis.

"You sure you wanna do this, 'cause if you want I'll just get his address and…"

"I wanna do it. He needs to think about what he did and he needs to face me. Believe me, you will be involved, but I wanna take my time with him. He already accepted my friend request, so my plan is in motion."

Zy's fingers softly grazed my back. "Okay. Whatever you wanna do baby. You know I got you."

I knew that he did and that was why I was willing to accept him as the man that he was. Finally I wasn't dwelling on what my mother had told me when I was younger, or what she felt like my fate should be. I was the one who controlled my destiny and there was no doubt in my mind that being with Zy was part of it.

"I know baby." I kissed his soft lips.

"Damn Baby. Since you been openin' that thang up for a nigga you been givin' me the business. That shit be havin' my toes curlin' and shit." He kissed my neck.

I giggled. "Oh really? You like that shit huh?"

"Love that shit," he whispered in my ear.

My body shivered and then was covered in goosebumps. He just had that effect on me and I enjoyed the feeling of loving him and being loved in return. Yeah, he was a street thug according to what he did to make money, but in my eyes he was the most sensitive, caring man I'd ever met. I loved that he was attentive and actually listened to me. Every night he came home to me and after he fulfilled his street duties he was all mine. Even if I had fallen for a straight laced man, there would be no guarantee that he'd have a heart of gold like Zy's. Roderick Lewis had a professional career, but he molested young girls. Zy could murder a million men and still be a better man than him in my eyes.

So, I laid there in my man's arms and thought about how I was going to feel when I'd finally exacted my revenge. Would I feel better or would it not change anything? It was a possibility that I would feel worse, but that was unlikely. The thought alone made me smile. After I took care of him it was on to Nina. Once they were both victims of my wrath I'd be able to concentrate on getting my degree and having a future with my man.

Chapter 13

Zyon

When I got up the next morning there was a note from Mackie on my pillow. It was only a little after eight AM, so I wondered where she was. Before I got up I picked up the piece of paper to read it.

Morning Babe,
I went to campus to handle my financial aid and other paper work. I'm thinking about going to summer school. In the meantime here's the poem that I was working on. I love you.

Baby

Zyon: My King, My Love

Milk chocolate skin tone
stretched over strong bones.
Women smile and sigh as they
stare into pools of sexy, light brown eyes.
You know that you got a queen at home, so you see
pass the flesh, because
you know that it's a test.

See, chaos has been the theme
of your scheme.
Having the desire

to seek a higher power.
You find faith in the unseen.

After it's all said and done,
the streets are fun, but
Now the future is looming,
and your life is blooming.
You may sell drugs,
and live the lifestyle of a thug,
but you somehow seem to sweep all of the nonsense
under the rug for love.

You still admire the opposite sex,
but now you think of what comes next.
Having been through the circumstances
of roller coaster romances.
Now it's not about infatuation,
but admiration.
Because you found a woman
that is strong,
who holds her own.

You see that the calm comes after the storm,
and tranquility becomes the norm.
Peace of mind supersedes
the constant grind.
Education is the key
to your situation.
Bettering yourself is
your wealth.
Not your money, not material things.
With me you have the chance to spread your wings.

Our love is the key
And our union will be blessed.
The two of us are destined for success.

As you watch our children grow
you know
deep down inside that
they will swell your pride.

This journey called life
is filled with strife,
smiles and ups and downs,
but through it all you
wear your crown.
Because you're my man.
My black king,
doing his thing.

All I could do was smile as I thought about my strong, black woman. She didn't need no financial aid though. I had to talk to her about that. I wasn't for her having loans and all that bullshit. Nah. I was going to pay my baby's tuition. I dialed her number to tell her to skip the financial aid shit and her phone went to voicemail. I sent her a text.

I loved the poem Baby. Call me okay. I don't want you gettin no loans and shit. You don't need financial aid. I got you. You know that.

After I sent the message I waited a few minutes to see if she would respond. When my phone rang, I just knew that it was her calling me back.

"Hey babe," I said not bothering to even look at the phone.

I was so busy looking up at the damn scores from the basketball games the night before.

"That's what's up. Now you know what the fuckin' deal is!" Kia's annoying ass voice rang loudly in my ear.

"Damn, what the fuck? I should've changed my number bitch. I thought your ass was finally over it!"

I wasn't in the mood for her ratchetness.

"So, your bitch is goin' to Spellman huh?"

"Why the hell you wanna know and what did I tell yo' hoe ass about disrespectin' my girl?" I really wondered how she knew that, but I wasn't confirming shit.

"I'm down here wit' my cousin and I saw her. Security had the place wrapped up, so I ain't fuck wit' the hoe."

"So it's somebody in your family who's smart enough to go to college?" I had to laugh at my own clever reference to how dumb she was.

"Fuck you nigga. Just for that I should go hit her in the back of the head wit' something. That bitch ain't wit' her now. Try me if you fuckin' want to!"

"Touch my girl again and you gon' get hit in the back of your head wit' something bitch!" She just didn't know that I could back up my threat.

"I'm sick of your threats Zy!"

"And I'm sick of yours. Leave my fuckin' girl alone and you won't have to worry about me actin' on 'em. All I want is for you to miss me wit' the bullshit. My girl ain't goin' nowhere, so you get used to that you slut bitch! Now go choke on a dick, I got better shit to do!"

Before I could hang up she had to say some shit that caught my attention.

"Them niggas Cam and Duke wanted to merk your ass at the strip club that night, but Ro was the one who had the heart to try nigga! You better watch your mufuckin' back before you be the one to get hit in the head wit' something. Choke on that shit muthafucka! You slippin' while you all in love wit' that boogie ass hoe! She got you all outta touch wit' the streets! Fuck you!"

She hung up and left me stunned as I stared at my phone. So Cam and Duke were with that nigga at Magic City. Obviously she was still fucking with Cam or how would she have known that. So those niggas had been hating the whole fucking time. Shit, it was just too bad that I wasn't slipping like that bitch Kia thought. The truth was that those scary ass niggas hadn't even given me a clue that they were on some hating type shit. I was just waiting for Mouse to confirm that he'd deaded both of those muthafuckas.

Baby called me back a few minutes later.

"Well, I guess I should get used to you doing for me, so I got out of the Financial Aid line. It was long as hell anyway."

"Where you at now?" I asked hoping that she was leaving Spellman's campus before she could run into Kia.

"I'm in the car now. You need anything before I get there?"

"Nah. Look, Kia just called me and shit. She saw you and well…just watch your back ma," I said with a sigh.

Shit, I felt bad as hell that she had to deal with Kia's drama. Why the hell couldn't that bitch just let go? Obviously she wanted Cam and he wanted her too. What the hell was she holding on to me for?

"I'm sick and tired of feeling like I have to watch my back Zy. Damn, if I ain't sent for the bitch why's she coming for me so hard. Hmm, I guess it's time for me to send for her ass! It's time I show that bitch so she'll know not to fuck wit' me!" She was fuming and I was tempted to get in my car, go find that heifer Kia and choke her to death myself.

"Nah ma. It's not the time nor the place. Your degree is more important than that dumb ass bitch. Come on to the crib. I'm good a'ight. All I want to do is see you right now."

She didn't say anything for a while.

"Baby?"

She cleared her throat. "I'm still here. I was just thinking. Shit, fuck it. A'ight. I'm on my way there."

*   *   *

After Baby got to the crib I loved up on her of course, but I had to head out to pick something up. She was knocked out when I left, and I figured that she'd still be asleep when I got back. All I had to do was make one stop anyway.

She didn't even move when I slipped out of the bed and got dressed. When I pulled up to my jeweler Manuel's store located in Buckhead on Piedmont Rd., I turned the engine off and made my way inside. It was after ten pm, but we had an appointment. Money talked, so he made sure that he made moves for me.

"Zy, what's up man?" Manuel asked as he gave me a gangsta hug.

"Ain't shit. Just tryna make it. How you been my nigga?"

Manuel was Middle Eastern and probably no more than thirty years old. He was up on hip hop culture, so in my eyes he was just a nigga with an accent. He was cool, so when we chopped it up, it was some real shit.

"Good man. You know how it is," he said as he led me into his office in the back of the store.

After he closed the door he sat down behind his desk and opened a drawer.

"I told you I could engrave anything," he said as he passed me a small, black velvet bag with drawstrings.

I opened the bag and emptied the contents in the palm of my hand. As I examined his handy work, I had to admit that I was satisfied.

"Hell yeah you did." I put it back in the bag and placed it in my pocket.

"So, you good man?" Manuel asked. "I mean, that shit's meant for somebody and well, I want you to be one hundred...."

"I'm gon' be good. My girl loved the bracelet too man. Good lookin' out," I said as I got up.

He shook my hand and nodded. "Anytime. You know how we do."

"Hell yeah. I gotta get back home to my ol' lady, so I'll see you when I come back for that other charm."

"Gotcha," he said as he got up to walk me to the door.

After I walked out he locked the door behind me and I headed to my ride. The late night traffic whizzed by as I got behind the wheel. I could remember a time when I'd be out partying or doing some dumb ass, reckless shit with my niggas. Now I was thinking about ways to keep my lifestyle intact. Duke and Cam were a threat, Kia was out of control and I couldn't find the first man I'd ever wanted to kill.

Something told me that what was going on around me was just the beginning. All of the shit that could hit the fan would rear its ugly ass head right when I'd fallen in love. Having feelings for someone other than myself made it a little bit harder to make decisions that could possibly end my life. No matter what, I had to think about the people who loved me. That included not only Baby, but my Pops and brother. Not only was killing Caruso important to me, but building those relationships was too, so I felt like I was caught between a rock and a hard place.

As I hit the gas and headed toward the highway to get back to my woman, I thought about the fact that I still hadn't heard anything back from Mouse. I dialed Deniro's number and he answered on the second ring.

"What's up D? You still ain't heard nothin' from that nigga?"

He knew who I was talking about. "I was just 'bout to call you man. I just got off the phone wit' Mel. He got word that Mouse was killed and shit. I got a feelin' that he tried to kill them niggas, but they came at him harder than he expected. Duke and Cam a'ight from what I know."

"What the fuck? Shit!" I yelled and hit the steering wheel over and over again in anger.

Duke and Cam were still alive and at that point I didn't know what they were capable of. Would I have to worry about who else was being shady and shit within my own fucking crew? Who the fuck could I trust if anybody? As far as I was concerned I didn't know who was loyal to the Cues and who was just there for the money and street fame.

"We gotta regroup man and come up wit' a fuckin' plan B. Them mufuckas can't be trusted and we gotta make sure they don't fuck up what we all worked so hard to fuckin' build. Diablo and Unc ain't gon' sit back and just watch what their blood, sweat and tears built crumble down around them. It's on now and I ain't gon' rest till them fuck niggas stop breathin'!" Deniro was passionate about the Cues and so was I.

"Already my nigga. Damn." I was still trying to process that shit. I just knew that Mouse had done the deed and the situation with Duke and Cam was one that I could move on from. "That bitch Kia told me that Duke and Cam was at the club, but Ro was the only one brave enough to step to me. Them niggas gotta be dealt wit' man. I'on know who else was fuckin' wit' them niggas."

"Me, Cane and Mel gon' shake them niggas up and see what we can find out. We still tryna find out who shot at that nigga. Somebody knows something, so it's only a matter of time before we find out what the fuck is up," Deniro said.

"A'ight man. Just hit me up tomorrow and shit. It aint nothin' we can do about those mufuckas right now." Caruso, Duke and Cam were all still targets that I couldn't get to.

*   *   *

Mackie

I woke up the next morning to an empty bed again. Zy had left in the middle of the night, but he came back and cuddled with me, so I figured that he had been out handling some business. I would've thought he was up to no good if he had ran straight to the bathroom for a shower, or smelled like he'd just taken one. The truth was that I did trust him. He had never given me a reason not to. At first I didn't trust him at all, but he'd earned it.

It just pissed me off that Kia was still interfering in our relationship. I'd avoided a confrontation with her at Spellman, but I knew that it was bound to happen again. Atlanta was a big city, but it was also a small world. Holding so much in over time made me want to go off. Between my memories of what happened to me as a child, the stress of Zy's lifestyle, the drama with my mom and life in general, I felt like I was a ticking time bomb. It was only a matter of time before I exploded. If Kia fucked with me or called my man one more time she was going to be the one to catch it when I snapped.

It was already two fifteen and I had asked Ayanna to meet me at The Cheesecake Factory on Peachtree Rd. Without my mother around to get advice from, I needed some from somebody. I would've talked to Princess, but I didn't want her to tell Tre that I was having issues with Zy's ex. Besides, Yanna was Zy's father's wife, so who was better to talk to?

My phone vibrated on top of the table and I saw that it was Yanna's calling. I was hoping that she wasn't going to cancel on me. I needed some good, solid advice and I needed it fast.

"Hey Yanna," I answered anxiously.

"Sorry, I was caught in traffic, but I'm parking now," she said sounding apologetic.

"It's no problem at all. I'll see you when you get inside. Oh, and it's the Braswell party."

"Okay. See you in a minute hon."

A few minutes later I spotted her walking toward me. At 5'3, she looked much taller in heels. She had that obvious pregnant woman's glow to her caramel colored skin, but she still wasn't showing yet. We greeted one another and hugged. When she sat down she removed her over sized designer shades and sat them on top of the table. Her hazel eyes twinkled as she smiled.

"So, what's going on chica?"

I smiled nervously. "I just need your advice about something."

She gave me a look of understanding as she nodded. "Okay," she said after sipping the water that was in front of her on the table.

Before I could say anything else, our server Denise came over to introduce herself as she sat a bread basket on the table. We told her to give us a little time before taking our order, because we were both undecided.

"Uh, before we get to the point, I must say that you don't look pregnant at all," I said as I scanned the menu.

"Thanks," she laughed. "I'm only nine weeks, so I'll be showing soon enough."

"I can't wait until I get to experience motherhood," I mused. "I'm gonna take my time though."

"Yes honey. You're young. Have fun," she said as she closed her menu.

I guess she knew what she wanted to order, but I still didn't. Honestly I didn't really have much of an appetite. As she spread butter on a piece of bread, I filled her in on Kia and everything that had been going on with her since I had been with Zy.

"Mmm, girl, you're singing to the choir." Yanna rolled her eyes toward the ceiling as she took a bite of her bead. "I fought so many bitches over Diablo I should be in the Guiness Book of World Records. Sometimes he was fucking them and sometimes he wasn't. It got to the point where it didn't make a difference. I'm older now and I'm a mother, but I still won't let some funky ass hoe disrespect me, or my man. Look, I'm not advising you to do anything crazy, but you have to do what you have to do to get that bitch off your back. Either that or leave Zy alone like she wants. Is that an option?"

I shook my head. "I know that he's not fuckin' her, so why should I leave him?"

"Exactly," she agreed. "But, sometimes a person may choose not to deal with the drama whether the person they're with is cheating on them or not."

"I don't want to deal with it, but leaving my man is not an option. It's just, well, what do I do to get rid of that heifer? Zy's already cut her off and that didn't make her go anywhere."

"You gotta scare that bitch away like she's tryin' to do you. Just know that most of those heifers who talk a lot of shit really ain't nothing but mouth. Like how she snuck you in the club. She'll talk shit, but when it's time to fight for real, she makes it so you're in the position not to fight back. Her lil' friend probably talked her into it.

She's tryin' to intimidate you into breakin' up with Zy, but once she see that you ain't going anywhere she'll back off. If she's really crazy, like some of the hoes that I've dealt with in the past, you may have to take drastic measures. Are you ready for that?" She gave me a serious look as I processed what she'd just said.

Before I could respond our server was back to take our orders. We both ordered quickly and got back to the conversation at hand.

"I don't know what I'm gonna do Yanna, but I'm ready for whatever. All I do know is how I feel about Zy. If he was cheating on me it would be different, but I know that he's not. I may sound naïve, but I know that he's not fucking that hoe. He's a good man and I want to be with him. I just can't help but feel like being with him has made my life change for the worst. Everything with him is good, but everything else isn't. My mom hates me and..."

Yanna cut me off. "What? Why would you think your mom hates you?"

She was munching on another piece of bread as I explained the argument between me and my mother.

"Well, I never had that problem. My mom wasn't there for me and my sister when we were kids because of drugs. She didn't give a damn who I was with, so your situation could be much worse. Just know that Sylvia loves you and she only wants the best for you. What she doesn't understand is that you're grown now and you have to decide what's best for you and what's not. She'll come around and when she does you have to swallow your pride and let her back in your life. You only get one mother Mackie and when she's gone it's no turning back. I lost my father, so my mother is all that I have. I decided to leave the past in the past. She will too because if what you and Zy share is real she'll see it."

I sighed. "I lost my father too. He was killed before I was born, so I never even had the chance to meet him. I hope my mom does come around, because I really miss her. We've always been so close and you're right. I want to patch things up with her, but she's the one who cut me off. What can I do?"

"Just be patient. That's what I had to do when it came to my mom. Don't force it. Just give her some time."

"Okay. Thank you so much Yanna. I mean, I know that we don't really know each other, but you still took the time out of your day to do this. I really appreciate it," I said gratefully.

She nodded and smiled. "You're like family, so it's no problem at all."

*   *   *

Before I got home from the restaurant I got the call from Verizon for a job interview. I was so excited, but I decided to wait to tell Zy when he got home. In the meantime I wasn't going to bother him. We had spoken right before I left to meet Yanna. He hadn't told me much, but from what I gathered he was trying to figure out how to handle Duke and Cam.

It was getting stressful as hell for Zy and although he pretended that it wasn't, I knew that the uncertainty of it all was fucking with him. I was starting to wonder if he wouldn't be as stressed if he wasn't so worried about me. Something told me that the streets were a lot easier for him to handle before I was in the picture.

When I finally got to the penthouse I ran straight to my laptop to see if Roderick had inboxed me, well Kimberly. He had already accepted the friend request. See, I didn't want to reach out to him first. Then he would be suspicious. I needed him to initiate contact and then I could continue with my plan.

Just like I thought, the perverted bastard had pounced.

Roderick: Hi Kimberly? How are you?

Kimberly: Fine and u?

Roderick: I'm great. How was school today?

Kimberly: It was ok. Didn't you see the status that I posted about how much I hate school yesterday?

Roderick: Yes. Lol. That's the reason I asked. I saw that you had a bad day because one of your teachers took your cell phone because you had called your boyfriend.

Kimberly: Lol. I hate teachers and parents too.

Roderick: Well, if it makes you feel any better, I'm not a parent. What grade are you in and how old are you?

Kimberly: I'm thirteen and I'm in the eighth grade.

Roderick: Okay. Well, the teen years are pretty tough years to get through. In no time u'll be grown and wishing u were a kid again.

Kimberly: I doubt that. I can't wait to be grown.

Roderick: So, why would you be calling your little boyfriend while you're in class? I mean, doesn't he go to the same school as you?

Kimberly: No, he doesn't go to school. He's twenty three years old. I don't like little boys. I'm into older men.

Roderick: Oh really. ;-) So, is that why u sent me a friend request?

Kimberly: Yeah. I had a page before and my boyfriend made me delete it. I just created this new page and I saw your pic because I live in Richmond too. We broke up yesterday, so I'm free to do what I want. Guess he's my ex now.

Roderick: Ur very pretty Kimberly and u seem to be very mature for ur age. I'm sure u will find someone else. His loss.

Kimberly: So, how old are you? Can I call you Rod?

Roderick: Yes and I'm twenty five.

I couldn't help but laugh out loud because I knew that shit was a lie. He had to be at least forty because he was at least thirty back when I was living with him and his wife.

Kimberly: Ok. You got a wife Rod?

Roderick: No

Wow. Another lie just rolled from his fingertips so easily. It was clearly stated that he was married on his page.

Roderick: Well, I was married, but we're getting a divorce.

Kimberly: My parents got a divorce when I was six. My dad ain't really been around since then. It's okay though. I can take care of myself, so I don't need him.

Roderick: If I had children I would never turn my back on them.

I rolled my eyes and wanted to say that was because if they were girls he'd probably be fucking them. That nigga lacked any fatherly instinct and I doubted seriously that it would have mattered if Nina and I were biologically his. Thank God he didn't have any kids. I wondered just how many girls he'd violated over the years.

Kimberly: Well, I have to go Rod, but I'll be logged on again later tonight when my mom ain't lurkin.

Roderick: Ok, ttyl beautiful.

My skin crawled as I thought about what he must've been thinking as we messaged back and forth.

He just knew that he was talking to some fast ass thirteen year old who was fucking twenty something year old men. There he was old enough to be a thirteen year old girl's grandfather and he was flirting and telling her how beautiful she was. What the hell made a man want to violate someone who he should be protecting and keeping safe? What made a thirteen year old girl sexy to a forty year old man? That shit made me want to throw up. I had to stop him before he could hurt another young girl.

*　　*　　*

"Babe, are you down for a trip to Richmond in a few days?" I asked when me and Zy were all cozy under the cover in one another's arms.

"Oh, hell yeah ma. I told you I got you. Just let me know what you want me to do."

He trailed kisses along my neck, causing my skin to instantly tingle. It was really crazy how he could make me relax when I wanted to be all wound up. Zy was just so good for me. Even while thinking about Roderick I was as cool as a cucumber.

"He finally took the bait and inboxed me today. It's only a matter of time before he asks me to come see him. I want you to kill him and I want to watch you do it." A chill traveled up and down my spine, but I wasn't afraid.

He was silent for at least a minute. "You sure you wanna do that? I mean, I'll kill that nigga, but do you really wanna watch? You ain't never seen nobody get killed before have you?"

I cleared my throat as the memory I'd tried to suppress for years crept back into my mental. "Actually I have. When I was fifteen me and Bey were walking to the park and these dudes got into it over some money. One of the dudes just pulled the gun out and shot the other dude in the head right in front of us. I was fucked up about it for a minute, but this is different. Roderick deserves to die for what he did to me and so many other young girls. I don't even know it for a fact, but I'm sure he's done it again and again."

Zy held me tighter. "You've been through a lot and all I wanna do is make it better."

"And you will when you kill Roderick for me." Tears stung my eyes, but I willed them away. I was tired of feeling weak.

Deep inside I knew that I was strong, but I was also a very emotional person. Whatever I felt, I felt it to my core. Sometimes I saw that as a sign of weakness and

I knew that I had to work on my sensitivity level. Nobody got through life like that. It was better to not let so much shit get to me. It was time for me to be a vigilante. I couldn't really say villain, because Roderick was clearly the villain.

"What about the chick…uh…? What's her name?"

"Nina. I had found her on Facebook, but she deactivated her page. I don't even know her real last night. On Facebook she was Nina Sofine or something like that. I'll just have to take care of her later. Right now I feel like I can't move into my new place, start school or take on a new job until I know that Roderick is…" My words trailed off. "Maybe then the nightmares will stop and I can get some sleep."

"They may get worse Baby," Zy pointed out.

"Well, at least I'll know that he can't hurt anybody else."

"You seem like you got your mind made up, so just let me know when."

I sighed and turned over to rest my head on his chest. "I know that you have a lot of shit on your plate too with Duke, Cam and the fact that you can't find Caruso, but I really need you for this."

He kissed my forehead. "I don't give a fuck what I got goin' on ma. You're my top priority. Don't forget that."

I nodded. "Thank you Zy. As crazy and farfetched as this shit may seem to others, I knew that you'd understand. That's why you're the only one who knows about this. I haven't even told Bey about what Roderick and Nina did to me."

"I love you ma and I'll go to hell and back for you. At the end of the day you gotta do what's gonna give you peace of mind. If you can live wit' it you know I can live wit' it, but I'll be glad to kill that nigga while you wait in the car. I mean…"

"I'll be right there so I can stare into his eyes and make sure that he takes his last breath. I need to see it and know that he's dead for a fact Zy. Okay."

"Okay Baby. Okay."

I was wondering what he was thinking.

"Do you think I'm crazy? I know that you are attracted to me because I am supposed to be so different from what you see around you all the time. This probably makes you feel differently about me. The fact that I want to see you kill him, I mean."

"Nah ma. I don't think you're crazy. I just think you're hurt and angry and you want revenge. No matter what you do, you're still different Baby."

Next thing I knew he was snoring and I'd finally drifted into a peaceful sleep for a change.

Chapter 14

Mackie

A week had passed since I'd had pillow talk with Zy about killing Roderick. I think he thought I'd change my mind about wanting to watch him do it, but I hadn't and I wasn't going to. I was moving the following week and my job interview was the week after. A week after that I'd be in summer school. All I wanted to do was be able to focus.

Then I was worried about Zy's situation. So far nothing had popped off and the police hadn't raided any of their spots or anything. Still, only a short amount of time had passed and getting warrants took time. I prayed everyday that my baby would be in the clear because he was never really physically involved in any of the drug deals. All I could was pray that no murders could be traced to him. It was a fact that he had lots of money, but thankfully Diablo had put a few of the businesses that Uncle Pete had passed down to him in Zy's name too. That way he had an explanation for his lavish lifestyle.

"Baby, I saw a hot ass Bugatti Veyron on the lot the other day. It was black and gray. Man that shit can go from zero to two hundred and fifty miles per hour in no time. Not only that, but you can brake at two hundred and fifty miles in ten fuckin' seconds. Dayum!" He was practically yelling.

I had heard every single word he said although I was typing away on my laptop. Roderick was trying to get me to give him my number. Giving him my real number was not a good idea and I didn't want to talk to him over the phone. It would possibly be given away in my voice that I hated him with a passion. Maybe I'd talk to him briefly after we scheduled a time to meet.

"A Bugatti? Don't you think that would be a bit much? A million dollar car is too damn flashy babe. You're already worried that the cops are going to be on your ass if Duke or Cam starts talking. It's no need to give them any ammunition. I mean, I know that you have businesses in your name, but don't start flexing and shit. It's not a good look and you know it. Get something a little less…you know…"

"Aww babe, you're too damn practical. We only live once and I can afford to get a Bugatti. Put it this way. I'm gonna test drive it when we get back from Richmond and if it don't feel right, I won't buy it."

I laughed. "Yeah right. You know that shit's gonna feel right."

He chuckled and then glanced over at the computer screen to see what me and the perv were talking about.

"That nigga is the worst. How the fuck you gon' dedicate your time to mackin' to a teenager and you a grown ass mufuckin' man. That mufucka's dick must be little as hell. Fuckin' nut case. I can't wait to put a bullet in his fuckin' head." Zy shook his head and I felt where he was coming from because I felt the same exact way.

"He wants to meet. Read this." She scrolled up and then pointed.

Roderick: I'm ready to see u. How about u come over this weekend? U have a curfew? If so we could see each other early.

Kimberly: I do have a curfew, but I'll tell my mom I'm spending the night with a friend. U gotta gimme the address.

Roderick: Lol. U won't talk to me on the phone, but u gonna come see me? Yeah right.

"He's skeptical. You gon' have to talk to him babe, but we ain't gon' give him your number. Give him the number for my burner phone. It can't be tracked and shit. If he ask why you got a Atlanta number tell him that you got a Google Voice account so your mama can't get a record of your calls," he advised.

I knew that he was right. If Roderick couldn't hear my voice he probably wouldn't be down for the visit.

"Okay, what is the number?"

He gave me the number and I typed it. Of course Roderick asked why I had an Atlanta number and I gave him the explanation that Zy had given me. He bought it and I was relieved. In no time he had sent me his home address. He claimed that he was separated from his wife, so I guess he didn't mind inviting me to his home. That was such a stupid move.

After that we wrapped our conversation up and he promised to call me in a couple hours. My flesh crawled at the thought of hearing his voice again, but it was going to all be worth it in the end.

"You okay Baby?" Zy asked in concern as he rubbed my tense shoulders.

"Yeah, I'm fine." My voice was barely audible and he could see right through my attempt to throw him off.

"No, you're not. I can see it in your eyes. You don't wanna talk to him. Look, if you want me to handle that nigga I will. You don't even have to go. Shit, I got his address now. All you gotta do is give me the word." His hands moved to rub my neck soothingly.

Damn, that shit felt good, but it wasn't really relieving my stress.

"No. I'm going with you. I don't wanna talk to him, but I'm gonna talk to him. If you go and do it without me, I'm gonna regret not facing him one last time. I have to do it for my peace of mind Zy."

He sighed. "I just don't see a person as sensitive as you gettin' any peace of mind from watchin' somebody die."

I pulled away from his touch and turned to look him in the eye. "You just don't know how much peace of mind I'm gonna get from watching *him* die. I'm not as sensitive as you may think. I hope this doesn't disappoint you, but sometimes I don't think I'm really that sensitive at all. It just so happens to be a fact that I love you and so you and the other people I love get to see that side of me. I don't have that same sensitivity toward someone who hurts me and Roderick is at the top of the list of people who have hurt me."

"So, what you tellin' me is that you ain't as sweet and innocent as I think?" A sly smile spread across Zy's face that made me laugh.

"That's exactly what I'm telling you? Maybe Kia was right about that, but it's not an act. I'm a good person, but I'm also the type of person who is tired of being fucked over. I think I have a friend like Bey and a boyfriend like you because I'm a lot more like you two than I ever thought."

"Hmm, that's real shit. I feel you ma. I do. Honestly, I ain't never really thought you were all that innocent and sweet at first. Shit, my first impression of you was damn, Baby is feisty. The more I get to know you the more I see that you can hold your own." He narrowed his eyes at me. "A woman like you is calculating as hell. You allow people to think you're all sweet and naïve because you're the total opposite. Instead you're strong and fearless. If you're pushed you can even become venomous. When a person underestimates you they'll get a surprise for that ass. There are predators out there in the wild who attract their prey by lookin' all pretty and innocent. I like that shit ma. For real. Yeah, I picked the right woman; a chameleon who can adapt to any situation."

I nodded in agreement. "Exactly."

He kissed my lips and then held me close. "You wanna get outta the crib for a lil' while?"

I nodded. "What you got in mind?"

"Well, I was thinkin' about a romantic dinner for two at Chops and then a movie or something. You know, something simple since it's a week night," he suggested.

"Sounds good." Then I remembered the impending phone call from Roderick. "Oh, but *he's* supposed to call me remember?"

Zy nodded and kissed my hand. "We can still go. If he calls you can just keep it short and sweet. Tell him that your mom's callin' your name or something."

"Okay, let's go. I love Chops."

*   *   *

We had just left Chops Lobster Bar and were headed to the movie theater when Zy's burner phone rang. It was a Richmond number, so I knew that it was Roderick.

"It's him, turn the music down," I said in a hurry.

Zy turned the music down and I pressed the button to answer the call.

"Hello."

"Hi Kimberly." I heard his familiar voice and my body instantly felt like it was on fire.

There were no nerves like I thought there would be. I only felt anger and the overwhelming desire to see him take his final breath. I hated him with a passion and the sound of his voice made those emotions feel raw all over again.

"Hi Rod. You finally called. I thought you wasn't serious about seein' me."

He was on speaker phone so Zy could hear the whole conversation.

"Oh, I'm serious sweetheart. I bet that you are even prettier in person."

I let out a flirtatious laugh as I rolled my eyes. "You'll see soon. I can't wait. I hope you like me."

"I know that I'll like you baby." My body trembled because I could remember how he would say baby to me. It felt and sounded so different from when Zy would say it.

"I have to go Rod. My mom's callin' me. Can we talk tomorrow?" I asked keeping the conversation as innocent and short as possible.

I couldn't fathom the thought of having a sexual discussion with him. Although I wasn't thirteen for real, I didn't want to think about having that kind of conversation with him. That shit really made me want to throw up in my mouth. It was something that I couldn't avoid though. We both knew his intentions, so it had to be discussed eventually.

"Okay sweety. I'll be thinking about you," the creep said.

I could tell that he was smiling and shit like planning to have sex with a thirteen year old was normal shit that a middle aged man did. If he had been put behind bars a long time ago, it would've saved a lot of heart ache and pain. Being that he hadn't been punished by the law, street justice would be served to his door very soon.

"And I'll be thinkin' 'bout you too."

"Oh, before you go. Uh, I was just wondering if I should get...condoms...or drinks or anything when you come?"

Oh my God, I thought to myself. The perv wasted no time initiating sex and trying to get a young girl drunk.

Zy shook his head, but managed to stay quiet.

"Yes, have condoms and some sour apple Smirnoffs," I said in a sweet, innocent voice.

I guess he'd graduated from molestation to consensual sex with teenage girls. Maybe he still did both. When I thought about it Nina must've allowed him to do things to her since she was so in love with him. Either way he was a sexual deviant who needed to be stopped.

"Okay, well we'll talk tomorrow."

"Okay," I said and hung up before I cussed his ass out.

"What the fuck? I can't wait to blast that fool!" Zy yelled angrily.

I couldn't wait either.

*   *   *

Zyon

Over the next few days Baby reeled that nigga Roderick in by pretending to be down to be with him. She'd even asked him if she could move in with him because she hated her mom and he agreed to it. He was referring to her as "his girl". That shit was downright sickening. He'd even asked her if she would pose nude or possibly let him record her. If he would ask her that he'd done that shit before. I was ready to take a road trip to kill that muthafucka.

In the meantime I was meeting up with my niggas to discuss how to get rid of the threat of Duke and Cam snitching, or putting a hit out on a nigga from behind bars. At that point none of us really had an update on the situation. My pops had hollered at Reco and he told him that he hadn't really been fucking with Duke like that.

"Reco said he and Duke kinda grew apart and shit since he made the choice to step down and get married. As far as he's concerned he's neutral 'bout the situation. He said do what you gotta do young blood," Diablo had told me earlier that day when we took Peanut out to eat and to the gym to shoot some ball.

"Pops know mufuckas," I spoke up knowing what plan b was, but those niggas didn't.

"Shit, we know that shit," Mel said with a laugh. As always that nigga was rolling a blunt of some good.

"Yeah nigga, tell us some shit we don't know," Deniro added.

Cane was unusually quiet, but he had been ever since that shot gun shell had taken off a chunk of meat from his shoulder. If the shell had actually entered his body the damage would've been a lot worse. More than likely he would've been dead. I guess he was more concerned with finding out who had bust at him and Bey. That nigga was hell bent on revenge and I knew that he was serious about fucking up the lives of whoever those niggas were.

I pulled an envelope full of Benjamins from the pocket of my True Religions.

"Make sure you take that shit to the address I texted you before I got here," I said to that nigga Deniro. "The nigga's name is Anthony. He go way back wit' Unc. He's a cop and shit, but he don't mind gettin' his hands dirty on the side if the price is right. He'll be transferrin' Duke and Cam to court on Monday. It's gon' be one other officer wit' him and he's up on game 'cause he gon' get his cut. They gon' set it up to look like them niggas tried to jump them, take their weapons, kill them and escape before they were forced to fill them wit' slugs."

Deniro nodded in approval and Mel passed the blunt to me.

"Sounds like a plan my nig," Mel said

I took a pull and glanced over at my nigga Cane. "What's up mane? You good?"

He nodded. "Yeah nigga."

"What's on your mind? You plottin' ain't you?" I asked and passed the blunt to him.

He took it and nodded. "Hell yeah. I think I know who ran up on me and my girl and shit."

"Who?" Deniro and Mel asked at the same time.

"I could've sworn I saw that bitch Ne Ne's Range behind me for a minute before I saw that van. Then when I looked again it was gone. I didn't see her behind the wheel or nothing, so I kinda dismissed the shit. Then earlier today I was on the block wit' that nigga Marco and he told me that he heard some foul shit in the streets. It's this new crew called the G Mob who call themselves tryna take over our blocks and shit. Their so called take over was supposed to start wit' knockin' off the top mufuckas on our side and then you Zy. Come to find out the nigga who run the G Mob is Ne Ne's fuckin' brother. From what the fuck I heard she had been holdin' that nigga off, well, up until I made a fool outta her ass. That bum bitch set me up and I got something for her ass and the fuckin' G Mob."

"When was you gon' tell us that shit nigga?" I asked suddenly feeling the urge to murder everything moving.

The Kings were out of the way and now some lame ass crew called the G Mob was gunning for a nigga's shine. Bullshit!

"Why the fuck you think I been quiet all this fuckin' time? I was waitin' for you to tell us about plan b and shit," Cane said with a look on his face that I couldn't read because I'd never seen it before.

"Well, I gotta handle some shit tomorrow, but I'll be back on Sunday. Ya'll niggas find out whatever you can 'bout them G Mob niggas." I shook my head as I stood up.

If it wasn't one thing it was another. My list of enemies seemed to be getting longer and longer. That shit didn't matter though. I wasn't going to stop ruling the streets of the A, nor was I going to be running scared because niggas wanted to see me dead. If them niggas wanted to bring it I was ready for war. The best way to show muthafuckas not to fuck with you was to make examples out of your adversaries. That shit was brewing in the streets of the A and I was going to make sure that it ended with the Cues still on top of the pyramid.

My ambition hadn't changed in the midst of all the chaos. I was still planning to take over the entire east coast with my raw, uncut product. We had that pure shit on reserve and I was going to flood the streets from Miami to Boston. Before I could even think that far, I had to handle the threats that were at home. In the meantime it was time to go to Richmond to kill a predator.

Chapter 15

Mackie

The ride to Richmond seemed to take forever although it was only about eight and a half hours. We had made a couple stops before checking into a nice hotel suite at the Doubletree. It was a little after five pm and I had told Roderick that I would meet him at six thirty at his house. The distance to his house was a thirty minute drive, so we didn't have much time.

"You ready for this?" Zy asked as he put the gun with the silencer on it in his jeans. The only reason that I knew that it was a silencer was because he'd told me earlier.

I wondered what type of gun it was, but I didn't ask. My fascination with guns was growing the more I spent time with him. Somehow I'd get the nerve to ask him to teach me how to shoot. I didn't want to give him too much of the new me at a time. Honestly, if I knew how to handle a gun, I would've volunteered to kill Roderick myself.

"I'm more than ready," I said as I stood on my tip toes to kiss him.

The truth was that my heart was about to beat out of my chest. Suddenly it crossed my mind that it was a possibility of us getting caught. What if the police stopped us on the way back to the hotel and found the gun? What if a witness saw us leaving the crime scene and reported the make and model of the car?

Zy had reassured me that everything was fool proof. He had a silencer on the gun so that no one would hear the gun shot. The car, which was an unassuming Black Honda Civic, had been reserved under a fake name and the room was too. The tags on the rental were dummy tags that he had got from Ju. Ju was married to Yanna's sister Maya and owned a detail shop. Of course he did a little under the table shit at times. In this day and time who didn't?

Before we had left to go to Roderick's I called him. He had insisted on picking me up somewhere, but I told him that he only lived a couple blocks from my friend's house and it would be best if I walked. Of course he agreed to that nonsense. How desperate was he for some young ass? Sicko.

"Hi Rod. My mom just dropped me off at my friend Kelly's. I'll be there in about thirty minutes," I said keeping up with my role as Kimberly as best I could. Did I tell him that my friend's name was Kelly?

"You sure you want to walk. I mean, I can come pick you up somewhere," he insisted.

"No, like I said before it's best that I walk. You wouldn't want anyone to see us in your car together would you?" It was sad that the supposed thirteen year old girl was smarter than him.

He chuckled. "You're right. Okay. I'm looking forward to seeing you and I didn't forget your sour apple Smirnoff."

I bet he didn't forget the condoms either. I ended our call and looked up at Zy.

"Let's go. I'm ready to get this shit over with."

*   *   *

We pulled up a few houses down from 2113 Grove Avenue. The house that Roderick lived in was beautiful and looked a lot more expensive than the one I had lived in when I was nine. Damn, he must've been doing even better than he was back then. The white two story Victorian style house looked like a woman lived there with all kind of green plants surrounding the place. I wondered where his estranged wife lived now. Mrs. Lewis had been smart if she made the choice to leave him.

Zy stayed behind me as I made my way up the steps of Rodericks home. He was careful to stay out of sight so that he wouldn't see him. The plan was for me to somehow unlock the door, so he could just walk right in. We both hoped that he wouldn't access a security alarm. In the case that he had one, I was advised by Zy to distract him so that he wouldn't set it. I was on it.

My nerves started to really get bad when I rang the doorbell. All types of thoughts were going through my mind, but none of them were remorse or second thoughts. My adrenaline was rushing as I watched Zy crouch down behind the bushes so that Roderick wouldn't see him when he opened the door.

Finally the door swung open and I was face to face with the monster who had hurt me when I was just an innocent little girl. He looked the same and didn't appear to have changed much. It was clear that he didn't recognize me and had no idea that I was nineteen instead of thirteen. Shit, most thirteen year old girls looked like they were older than me nowadays anyway.

"Kimberly, you made it," he said trying to sound all sweet and caring. Yeah right.

I managed to flash a fake ass smile at him. Zy had given me a switchblade knife just in case I needed it. He told me to scream if that nigga did anything crazy and he'd bust the window open to get in there. I just hoped he'd get in before anything like that popped off.

"Yes, I told you I was coming."

He nodded and stepped aside for me to come inside. I watched him lock the door behind us before leading me into the living room. He hadn't set an alarm though, so that was a relief. We sat down on the black leather sofa and the first thing he wanted to do was offer me a drink.

"So, how about one of those Smirnoffs? I want you to relax. I mean, you will be spending a lot of time here, so we may as well get acquainted." He had a sick smile on his face and I couldn't stand to even look at him. Fuck getting acquainted. I was there to get even.

"Yeah, a Smirnoff would be good. Damn, I should've asked you if you got some weed too," I said for good measure.

"I swear, ya'll girls are way more advanced now than when I was growing up. I met my ex wife when she was your age and she was nothing at all like you."

I wished he'd go ahead and leave the room so I could open the door for Zy. Instead he decided to sit beside me and put his hand on my knee.

"You smell really good," he said leaning all close to me.

I could smell his breath, so I held mine, because his smelled like raw garbage. No wonder he was into little girls. No grown woman would deal with his stinking ass breath. I tried my best not to frown up my face. When he tried to kiss me I reminded him of my drink.

"Uh, before we get to that can I have my drink first. I mean, I did just walk three blocks and I'm thirsty." I was still smiling so he wouldn't take me interrupting his kiss the wrong way.

He laughed and blew that tart breath in my face again. Damn, I thought I was going to die right then and there, but I held it together.

"Oh, I'm so sorry sweet heart. I'll be right back. Oh and I do have some weed, so I'll roll us a joint. Make yourself at home." He winked at me and left the room.

I jumped up quickly and ran to the front door to unlock it. After zooming back past the beautiful modern art and sculptures that decorated the place, I was back on the sofa like I'd been there all along. Roderick came back with two Smirnoffs and sat down beside me. He had already removed the top and I wondered if he had put something in it. Damn, what the hell was taking Zy so long?

"Thank you," I said giving him a grateful smile as I waited for my man to rescue me. My mind was on that knife in my pocket. He had one more time to try to kiss me.

Just as I put the bottle to my mouth to pretend like I was going to drink it, he grabbed my crotch hard as hell.

"Now, we both know you didn't come here to drink watered down alcohol and shit. You know that you wanna fuck! Now take off your fuckin' clothes you little bitch!" His whole demeanor had changed and my mind flashed back to when I was nine.

Before I could grab the knife, stab him and scream, I heard the sound of Zy's voice behind me.

"Get yo' hands off her muthafucka and get your perverted ass against the wall!" He yelled.

Roderick slowly removed his hand from between my legs and put his hands up. He looked up at Zy with a confused look on his face.

"You the cops? What? Is this some Dateline bullshit?" He asked in shock as he looked at me.

"Nah nigga. I ain't the cops. I'm worse than the fuckin' cops. You wish that was all you had to worry about. I'm here to serve you death, not a fuckin' warrant muthafucka. Now, get the fuck up and get away from my woman!"

Roderick looked at me and got up from the sofa. As he leaned against the wall he asked, "What the fuck's going on?" His eyes were getting all teary and shit and I wanted to see him cry like a little bitch.

"You're finally gonna get what the fuck you deserve *Mr. Lewis*." I said his name mockingly.

He squinted his eyes at me. "Who the fuck are you?"

"Well, I'm not a thirteen year old girl named Kimberly and you're not twenty five either. I'm Mackienzie Braswell and I'm nineteen years old. When I was nine I was sent here to live with you and your wife. You came in my room every night and molested me for nine months. You ruined my life you son of a bitch!" I yelled. "So, I'm here now to end yours. I wanted you to look at my face one more time before you die so you can remember it for an enternity."

Tears suddenly fell from his eyes, but mine were dry. I refused to shed a single tear for his ass. He didn't give a fuck about my tears when I was a helpless little kid. Now he wanted to cry because there was a grown man holding a gun in his face; the gun that was going to seal his fate.

"Look, I'm so sorry about that okay! I need help. I'm a sick, sick man. I have a problem and that's why my wife left me. She...she..."

"Shut the fuck up muthafucka!" Zy roared loudly as he closed the distance between them.

I just stood there and watched as the scene unfolded with a satisfied smirk on my face. There was snot running out of Roderick's nose as the tears fell down his face like waterfalls. Those crocodile tears didn't move me or Zy. All they did was fuel the fire that burned deep inside of the both of us.

"I'm 'bout to show you a real man before you die! A real man don't fuck little girls muthafucka! A real man is man enough to face what consequences come from his actions! You knew you'd face karma one day nigga! You just didn't know that karma was gonna be a bad muthafucka like me! I'm man enough to look you in your face while I kill your ass. I could've easily put a bullet in you from a distance, but that's some weak, punk ass bullshit. Baby, didn't even have to take it this far. I just wanted to come kill your ass, but nah, she insisted that you know the reason before you die. I don't understand why since you gon' be dead anyway."

"Don't, no please don't!" Roderick continued to plead for mercy.

Neither of us had any.

"Where's your computer?" I asked as I scanned the room. "How many other girls have you taken advantage of Roderick Lewis?"

Roderick shook his head as he continued to cry. "I…I…I want some help. I really do. You don't have to kill me," he pleaded for his life, but it fell on deaf ears.

I spotted his laptop sitting on a small table in the far left corner of the room. "Hold up," I told Zy as I walked over to retrieve it.

I turned it on. "What's your password?" I asked turning to look at the grown man who was crumbling before my eyes.

He sniffed before answering. "Lewis1269."

I put in the password and the computer flashed to the home screen. The screensaver was innocent enough, so I glanced over the icons that were on the screen. When I found the one for Internet Explorer I clicked on it. Then I looked at the history of the websites that he visited. Just like I thought, that nigga was into kiddie porn. When I opened his picture file he had hundreds of photos of naked girls. Some looked to be as young as five and six.

"Kill that muthafucka," I said with tears falling from my eyes. I was crying for those little girls.

I didn't even bother to look away when Zy forced the gun into his mouth.

"No! No! No!" Roderick begged him not to shoot him, but that shit didn't matter to Zy.

One gunshot made his head erupt and his brain matter and bright red blood hit the wall. His body slid down in the sitting position and then his head slumped over.

Zy made his way over to me and took his shirt off. He used it to wipe off the computer so that my finger prints wouldn't be on it. He then wiped off the doorknob on the inside and outside of the house. He also made sure that he grabbed the Smirnoff bottle that I'd touched.

We left the computer on so that when the police came inside they'd see it. When they checked it they would find all of the evidence they needed to not even want to investigate his murder. I was sure that they would just chuck it up as another worthless pedophile that got what the fuck he deserved. On the way to the hotel Zy kept asking me if I was okay.

"I'm fine baby. Better than ever," I stated honestly.

At that point I was thinking about how I was going to find Nina and what I was going to do to her. Then my mind drifted to how I was going to get Kia's ass out of the picture once and for all.

*   *   *

Zyon

I was worried as hell about Baby, but when we got back to the hotel she seemed fine. After a hot shower, a much needed blunt and some Chinese food we were all laid up. She was the one who wanted to get all sexual. I had refrained from initiating sex, because I didn't know if she was in the mood. Obviously she was.

"I'm okay baby," she insisted. "So stop asking."

"Okay," I agreed to stop pestering her about it, but I didn't expect for her to start kissing down my abdomen to my hardening dick. "Damn."

"I have to show my gratitude somehow," she said in a sexy ass voice that made me even harder.

"You know I'll do anything for you ma,' I whispered with my hands in her hair.

"Mmm hmm," she moaned with her mouth full.

*   *   *

We were up the next morning by nine, but before we could check out of the room some breaking news caught our attention.

"The body of Roderick Lewis was found by his wife Tanya Lewis today in their home on Grove Street after she returned from a trip out of town. He suffered one fatal gun-shot wound to the head at close range. It appears to be an execution style homicide and authorities are investigating further to identify the motive. Mr. Lewis was a pillar of his community and served as a Deacon at his local church. He was also a well respected lawyer who often took on juvenile cases pro bono. His computer has been confiscated to aid in the investigation. His wife is not a suspect and is cooperating with police. There are no witnesses or suspects at this time. We will keep you updated as the investigation unfolds."

"So he wasn't separated from his wife," Mackie said as she shook her head. "I just hope they find out who he really was and expose him. Pillar of the community my ass. Get the fuck outta here."

"No. *let's* get the fuck outta here." I quickly gathered our belongings and we were on the way to the car.

Neither of us expected for his body to be found so soon being that he was supposedly not with his wife anymore. It was a good thing there were no witnesses, so we were in the clear. We'd be back in Atlanta soon anyway. Once we were back on the highway I felt more at ease. I just hoped Baby was okay for real.

I grabbed her hand. "You good ma?"

"Yeah babe. I'm good. When we get back to Atlanta I don't want you to ask me that okay. It's over now and I have the peace of mind that I wanted." She smiled at me and squeezed my hand. "At least I know that he'll never hurt another girl."

I nodded in agreement and turned the music up. As long as Baby was good, I was good. Still, the infamous life that I lived had niggas wanting to gun for me. I had to make sure I eliminated all threats to my life, before I could take Caruso's.

*   *   *

The next day Cane called to give me the word on the G Mob. "Those niggas ain't deep worth shit. We already know where they be at. We'll knock them off the map in no time. We got some niggas on watch, so they gon' give us the word when it's time to go in on them reckless ass fools."

"Bet that nigga. Just keep me posted a'ight?"

"A'ight."

It was already after six pm on Monday and I was waiting for my pops to let me know that he'd gotten the word that Duke and Cam were dead. When I saw his number pop up on the screen I answered without even letting the phone finish ringing.

"Sup Pops? What's the word?" I asked anxiously.

"No word on that just yet," he said disappointing me instantly. "That's gon' take a while. You know paper work and all that shit. We probably won't know shit 'till later tonight or tomorrow."

"Oh, okay. Damn. So, what's up then?" I asked knowing that it had to be something.

Baby was out picking out curtains and shit for her new crib and I was out and about handling shit as usual. I was sure to keep my eyes and ears open just in case a muthafucka wanted to try a nigga.

"I got word on Caruso," he said causing me to forget about anything else.

"So what's up?" I asked feeling a rush come over me.

"He's been hidin' out in Italy and shit, but he'll be back in Brooklyn next week. The thing is he'll only be there for one day. His favorite brother Saul is dying and of course he wants to say his farewells. They gon' sneak him in, but he won't make it back on that private jet," Diablo said menacingly.

Even I got chills when he said that shit.

*   *   *

When I got to the crib I went into my bedroom and opened the closet door. I reached up on the top shelf and grabbed my .44 revolver. As I held it in my hand I walked over to my underwear drawer and grabbed the little drawstring bag that I had got from Manuel that night I visited his jewelry store.

I emptied the contents in my hand and just stared at it. The bullet gleamed at me as I read the word

CARUSO over and over again. Manuel had engraved my number one enemy's name on a gold plated .44 bullet. That one bullet was going to finally put out that fire in me that had been burning for a decade. That was only one fire amongst many though. Killing Caruso wasn't going to end the war that had started right there in the A. I was going to end a turf war before I embarked on the mission in New York.

Until I did, staring at that bullet was enough. It was the motivation that I needed to keep my blood pumping another day. My love for Baby was also fueling my fire. There was no way that I could be the man she needed if I didn't get rid of the man who had taken away my first love. As I kissed that bullet, I looked up toward the ceiling.

"This one's for you ma."

The End!!!

About The Author

Nika Michelle is originally from NC and currently resides in Atlanta, GA. Her love for books started at a very young age and inspired her passion for writing. Blessed with a vivid imagination, she would share her short stories with her classmates in middle and high school. In 2002 she graduated from Fayetteville State University with a BA in Communications and English/Literature. During her time in college she completed her first novel "Forbidden Fruit", an urban tale that spins a web of love, lust and greed. Her other titles include Forbidden Fruit II: A New Seed, Forbidden Fruit 3: The Juice, Forbidden Fruit 4: The Last Drop, Forbidden Fruit 5: The Final Taste, Black Butterfly, Black Onyx: The Sequel to Black Butterfly, Black Magic: Book 3 of the Black Butterfly Series, Black Lace: Book 4 of the Black Butterfly Series, Zero Degrees 1, 2 and 3 (collaboration with Leo Sullivan), The Nookie Ain't Free, The Nookie Still Ain't Free, The Empress, Bout That Life: Diablo's Story (A Forbidden Fruit Prequel). Love In the A (A Forbidden Fruit Spin Off) and Love In The A 2: Thicker Than Blood. Love In The A 3: Bad Blood is dropping on Kindle April 13th!!

Available Now!!

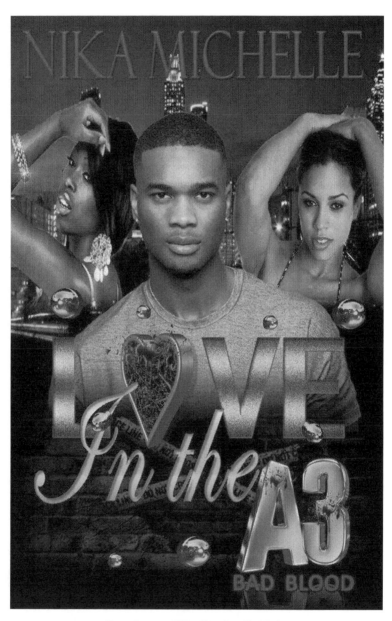

Coming to Kindle April 13th

Made in the USA
Lexington, KY
03 October 2018